GOOD INTENTIONS

ALSO BY BRANDON MASSEY

GOOD INTENTIONS

BRANDON MASSEY

DARK CORNER PUBLISHING

ISBN: 979-8-9854216-8-2 (paperback)

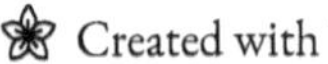 Created with Vellum

BEFORE

"Nate! Your friend is here!"

On that Friday afternoon in April, Nate Noble worked on his math homework in his upstairs bedroom when his mother called. Two days off from school lay ahead, and though he could have postponed the assignment, he wanted to complete all his obligations to free up his time for the weekend.

But his mom's voice shattered his concentration.

My friend? Nate frowned, a pencil clamped in his grip. *What if it's Marvin?*

Of course, it could *only* be Marvin, his best friend, who often visited in the afternoons after school to hang out.

Gnawing his bottom lip, Nate slipped on his sneakers and met his mother at the bottom of the staircase. Mom had arrived home from work a short while ago and still wore her business suit from her job at Georgia Power. Her burnished mahogany complexion bore traces of faded makeup.

"Is it Marvin?" Nate asked.

He hoped his voice would mask the anxiety coiled in his stomach like a knot of tangled wire. Was Marvin there because he'd discovered what Nate had done at school that day? Or was it an innocent visit?

"It's him," Mom whispered. "That boy's so quiet—won't say a word, just knocks on the door and stands there like a statue. He doesn't need to be afraid of me."

"It's not you," Nate said.

Tragic knowledge clouded his mother's penny-brown eyes. Yes, she knew who Nate meant. *We all went to high school together,* she'd once shared when speaking of Marvin's parents. *His stepdad was an asshole back then, too.*

"I feel bad for the boy," she said. "But we can't stick our nose into that family's business."

What would Mom think about what Nate had done? Would she approve? Or would she get angry?

You know what Mom would say—she just said it. We can't get into that family's business.

Nate shuffled past his mother and went to the door.

"We're going out for pizza in an hour," Mom said. "Don't ride off too far."

Marvin Waters stood on their front porch, waiting patiently. Nate and Marvin were twelve and stood about the same height, but Marvin's wispy build made him appear younger. He slouched, head bent, as if cringing from an invisible blow.

Marvin's Afro sprouted unkempt ridges and valleys. Nate's uncle owned a barbershop and trimmed Nate's hair into a clean fade every two weeks, like clockwork. Still, Nate never dared criticize Marvin's hair, unlike some other guys at school. Behind his back, other boys called Marvin "Chewbacca" after the furry *Star Wars* character.

The afternoon was unseasonably warm, even for Atlanta. Yet, Marvin still wore his Atlanta Falcons varsity jacket with the tarnished team logo, sleeves rolled up to expose his bony, hairy brown forearms.

But Marvin didn't look angry. Nate's tension drained away. He stepped into the humid afternoon.

"Hey," Nate said. "What's up?"

"Wanna go for a ride?" Marvin asked, his voice soft and tentative.

He barely met Nate's gaze when he asked—bracing himself for a "no," probably, even though they rode together a few times a week.

"Mom said I've got to be back in an hour," Nate said.

Nate didn't mention that he, his younger sister, and his mother were heading out for pizza. Once, he had invited Marvin, and Marvin shook his head in stubborn refusal, mumbling: "My dad won't let me go. I can't ask him."

Nate kept his Huffy BMX bicycle chained to the carport's thick wooden pillar beside their split-level house, where it stood next to his mother's Honda Passport. As Nate unlocked his bike, Marvin waited on his Huffy in the narrow asphalt driveway, staring at the ground as if it broadcast a vision of his future.

Although Marvin's quiet demeanor had initially reassured Nate, it confused him. Had anyone at the school even read his letter? Had they reviewed it and thrown it into the trash? Nate expected some reaction—a good reaction, he hoped—would have reached his friend by now.

But this was the same Marvin he saw daily: silent and intense. They had been friends since sixth grade, the start of middle school, and Marvin rarely had much to say when they were together. Their friendship revolved around activities. They rode bikes throughout the neighborhood, and they played *Donkey Kong* and *Mario Bros.* and sometimes other games on Nate's Super Nintendo. Marvin excelled at those games, and Nate suspected his friend had his own gaming console at home, but Marvin never admitted it. Marvin always came to Nate's house. Early in their friendship, Nate visited

Marvin's home to ask if he wanted to hang out, and Marvin's mom answered the door. She was a pretty but sad-faced, ebony-hued woman with tears glistening in her big, deep brown eyes, flanked by a diminutive child Nate recognized as Marvin's baby sister. Startled, Nate asked for Marvin, and his friend hurried outside to meet him.

Marvin had later warned him in a somber tone, "It's better if I come to see you. My mom is sick." That was the last time Nate had visited his friend's house or heard him speak of his mother.

But the wounds that occasionally surfaced on Marvin's slender body spoke volumes about his stepfather. Last week, when they changed into gym clothes for PE class, Nate spotted several cigarette-burn blisters on Marvin's briefly exposed, hair-fringed back. Marvin shrugged when Nate asked him what had happened, as if Nate didn't already know.

That was when Nate decided he had to act. He had once read a quote, "All it takes for evil to exist is for good people to do nothing," and those words resonated with him. He would do *something*.

Nate climbed onto his Huffy. They set off.

They pedaled without discussing their destination, but they usually ended up at the same place: a local park with a paved trail that wound through several acres of pristine, wooded land. Atlanta had evolved into a concrete jungle in many ways, especially with the Olympics coming to town in 1996. However, the city still had those ethereal pockets of green space that Nate loved.

"Wanna race?" Nate asked as they drifted alongside each other.

"Bet." Marvin's eyes flashed.

They took off.

Halfway to the park, as they raced along a tree-lined residential road a few blocks from the house, Nate heard a rumbling car behind them, the bassline from a popular rap song booming from the speakers.

Hairs lifted at the nape of Nate's neck. Before he turned to look, he knew who was coming.

Riding beside Nate, Marvin seemed to know, too: his pupils dilated, and he slowed as if sapped of energy.

A car horn barked. Nate winced and looked over his shoulder as the crimson Buick Regal pulled up alongside them.

The driver cut the music; the passenger window gaped open. Cigarette smoke poured from the car's interior, and Nate's stomach clenched.

Mr. Leon Waters, Marvin's stepfather, glowered at Marvin, smoke tendrils curling around him in the car as if he were on fire. Mr. Waters was a sharp-faced man with a reddish-brown complexion, a beard tapered to a fine point, and dark eyes like hollow-point bullet tips. He might have been handsome if he hadn't worn a perpetual scowl.

"Get your narrow ass in this car right now, boy!" Mr. Waters shouted. Like a demon summoning a soul to hell, he pointed at Marvin with the glowing cigarette tip.

Nate stopped pedaling his bike, but Marvin crawled forward. Nate couldn't believe it. Was Marvin *trying* to piss off his stepfather?

The Buick roared, jolted forward, and swerved to the right, front tires punching the curb—and cutting off Marvin's path.

Stalled, Marvin threw his head back and unleashed a primeval cry, his entire body shuddering. Nate had never heard anything like it in his life. It sounded like a howl of anguish or rage. Maybe both.

A chill raced down Nate's spine.

Mr. Waters leaped from the car and stalked toward Marvin. Nate had never seen someone move so fast. In one blink, the man was in the car; in the next blink, he descended upon Marvin, who froze in place like a cornered deer, silent again.

Mr. Waters stood about six feet tall, his frame packed with lean muscle. He wore jeans, a sleeveless white T-shirt, and scuffed boots crusted with reddish Georgia clay.

Before Nate knew what he was doing, he got off his bike and approached them. A protective instinct seized him. Mr. Waters terrified him, but Nate feared what might happen to Marvin if he did nothing to help his friend.

Mr. Waters whacked Marvin upside the head with a vicious, backhanded slap. Marvin took the hit without making a sound as if getting hit like that was expected.

"You heard me, you little motherfucker!" Mr. Waters snarled. "You come when I call you, boy!"

Do something.

"Get away from him!" Nate said.

His shout seemed barely above a whisper, but Mr. Waters pivoted to face him. The man's nostrils flared; it was easy to imagine steam pouring out of them.

Nate stood his ground, his chest heaving. Marvin trembled, shaking his head, silently mouthing the same word: *no.*

"Oh, you want some, too, little man?" Mr. Waters said. "I don't give a damn who your mama is. You disrespect me, and I'll light your ass up."

"Leave Marvin alone!" Nate said.

Mr. Waters stepped forward and shoved Nate in the chest as casually as a man brushing away a toddler. Nate stumbled backward, got tangled up in his own feet, and fell on the hard concrete, landing on his tailbone.

He bit his tongue. Warm blood gushed through his mouth.

Mr. Waters seized Marvin's arm and wrangled the boy to the passenger side of the car, flung open the door, and tossed Marvin inside. He slammed the door and turned on his heel, but not before he fired a warning glare at Nate.

"You ought to respect me, boy." Mr. Waters sneered. "Your mama ain't taught you shit about me, huh?"

Mr. Waters spat on the ground, slid into the Buick, and pulled away with a squeal of tires, foul exhaust fumes spitting from the tailpipe and fogging around Nate's head.

Nate shook, his chest aching from where the man had pushed him. Warm tears trickled down his face.

Was Marvin in trouble with his stepfather because of him? This wasn't supposed to happen. He was trying to save his friend—not get him in more trouble.

. . . we can't stick our nose into that family's business . . .

Marvin's abandoned Huffy lay against the curb. Someone might steal the bike if Marvin didn't come back to get it. But when would Marvin be back?

Nate groaned and got to his feet. He dragged the back of his hand across his tear-streaked face.

His butt ached from hitting the road, but it was nowhere near as bad as what Mr. Waters had done to Marvin. No one had ever hit Nate as brutally as Marvin's stepfather had smacked him, and Marvin hadn't made a sound.

He had to do something, but what could he do?

Get the bike, Nate. You can do that.

Nate climbed onto his bicycle, plodded to Marvin's Huffy, and lifted it by one of the handlebar grips.

Pedaling slowly, one hand grasping the middle of the other bike's handlebars, Nate transported Marvin's bicycle to his friend's house, about four blocks away. It seemed to take forever to reach Marvin's street. He dropped the bike a few times, swearing under his breath whenever he did so, but at last, Marvin's dark green, ranch-style house came into view at the end of the block, the yard bristling with weeds and thorny bushes.

The place looked abandoned, but the red Buick Regal sat in the dusty driveway. A wasp circled the car like a sentry.

You disrespect me, and I'll light your ass up.

When Nate reached the curb in front of the house, he got off his Huffy. He pushed Marvin's bike along the cracked walkway leading to the front door.

He thought: *I'll leave the bike near the porch and go. Then I'll head home and tell Mom what happened. Mom may know what to do, but she'll be mad that Mr. Waters pushed me.*

But what would he say when Mom asked him why Mr. Waters

had turned on him? *You stuck your nose into that family's business, didn't you, Nate? Didn't you start it all?*

As Nate neared the house, the bike jangling alongside him, he noticed something unexpected: the scarred front door hung open a few inches.

So what, Nate? You're not welcome here. Even Marvin told you that before.

And then, Nate heard the scream.

1

____

Thirty years later

"You're right on time, babe," Leslie said. "How was traffic?"

Nate had climbed out of his Chevy Silverado to meet his fiancée, Leslie Clark, in the driveway of the baker's house. A blanket of gray clouds hung low in the January sky, and a biting chill nipped at his skin. He reached inside the pickup to retrieve his windbreaker, the fabric cool and slick against his fingers as he slid it over his UPS Store uniform shirt.

"No issue," Nate said. "Is everything set for this cake tasting? I need to get back to Norcross by two. I have another interview to do—the last one, if all goes well."

He and Leslie exchanged a quick kiss, her lips soft and glistening with gloss. Leslie had come on her lunch break from her accountant job. Though Nate was his own boss, his schedule was far less forgiving than hers. This was their second attempt at the tasting; he'd missed the first appointment due to a work emergency.

"The table's set for us." Leslie grinned, her dark amber eyes gleaming. "Ready to eat cake?"

"I'm here, aren't I?"

Leslie's smile faded.

That came out wrong, he thought.

"Sorry," Nate said. He reached for her hand, her slender russet-brown fingers warm in his, her one-karat engagement ring pressing against his thumb. "It's been a rough morning, Les. Issues at every store."

"I know you don't want to be here." She gestured to indicate the nearby house. "I know you're not a fan of this fancy wedding stuff."

They had scheduled a May wedding, five months away. They'd planned for two hundred and fifty guests, a ceremony at her family's longtime Baptist church in southwest Atlanta, and a glitzy reception at a posh Buckhead hotel. Leslie was thirty-seven, and as her parents' only daughter, her family intended to spare no expense.

Nate preferred a much smaller affair: a private exchange of vows and a small reception dinner at a cozy restaurant. He'd been married once before, in his early twenties, to his college sweetheart—a disaster that lasted seven months—and he viewed the pomp and circumstance of a big event as a waste of time and money.

But Leslie was an amazing woman, and he felt fortunate to be with her. They'd lived together in his house in Lawrenceville for a year, but if he wanted to spend his life with her, he had to support her "Big Day." Cohabiting indefinitely wasn't an option, and Leslie told him she had dreamed of a blowout wedding since she was a teenager.

At least her parents were paying for most of it. He couldn't complain about the cost, but the constant intrusions on his time were another matter. As a franchisee with three busy UPS Stores under his umbrella throughout Gwinnett County, time was his most precious commodity.

"Let's head inside," Nate said.

The baker, Nicole, ran her home-based business from her spacious basement, which she'd converted into a full-scale kitchen and studio. The scents of vanilla, cocoa, and lemon swirled in the air, tempting and inviting.

As Leslie had promised, a presentation table awaited them, featuring several cake flavors on small plates, each one labeled: red velvet, vanilla with strawberry, vanilla with raspberry, lemon, and chocolate.

Nate and Leslie sat beside each other.

"They all look delicious," Nate said.

"Leslie says you love chocolate," Nicole said. She swept her hand above the table, highlighting the variety of slices. "If you select a different flavor for the wedding cake, you could have chocolate for your groom's cake at the rehearsal dinner. Just something to consider as you sample them."

Nate glanced at Leslie. "Do I need a *groom's* cake?"

"We've talked about this before," she said.

"We have?"

"Yes, we have." Her jawline tightened. "It's tradition, Nate."

The baker must have noticed Nate's dismay because she said, "You don't need to decide now, guys. Let's focus on your wedding cake for today, and we'll come back to that one later. Sound good, y'all?"

Nate picked up a fork. His mobile phone buzzed as he pulled the slice of red velvet toward him. It was an incoming call from his Norcross store.

"I need to take this," he said.

Leslie looked at him sourly but said nothing; she only plucked up her fork and reached for a slice.

Nate stepped toward a corner of the studio and accepted the call. It was the store manager, breaking news that he knew would upset Leslie.

A couple of minutes later, he returned to the table. Leslie was sampling slices and chatting with the baker in an animated voice.

His stomach knotted. He hated to ruin the day and be the bad guy again.

"I'm needed at the Norcross store," Nate said.

Leslie stopped speaking to the baker mid-sentence and stared at him.

"Why?" she asked.

"My manager has a family emergency and needs to leave. There's no one else there, Les. She's the only staff at the store today since someone called in sick."

"Can't you get someone else to fill in for her?" Leslie frowned. "What we're doing here is important."

"My other manager has the day off. I've got to respect their time."

"But no one respects *your* time."

"Welcome to business ownership. You're always on the clock. That's the life."

"But you control your schedule. You're the boss."

"Remember that old blues song? You pay the cost to be the boss."

Leslie rolled her eyes.

"It's hard to find good help these days." Nate slid on his jacket. "If I treat everyone well, give them flexibility and the benefit of the doubt, they'll give me their best effort."

"I appreciate that you've got good intentions with these folks, but you know what they say about good intentions and where they lead."

Nate waved off her remark. "I'm sorry. I've gotta go."

"Go on, then. I asked Nicole to pack the samples for you. I expected this would happen."

"That's why I love you." He stepped forward to kiss her.

She met his lips without enthusiasm. He knew he would hear more about this incident later. It was far from settled. Leslie was an understanding woman, but her patience had its limits.

Chalk it up as one more issue he had to figure out.

Twenty minutes later, Nate arrived at his UPS Store. It sat in the Peachtree Square Shopping Center off a busy stretch of Peachtree

Parkway, anchored by a Publix supermarket. After eleven months in business, the Norcross location was his highest-volume store, accounting for half of his projected gross annual revenue.

He'd taken out a significant loan and brought in an outside investor—Leslie's dad, ironically—to open this third location. Keeping the shop staffed and operating smoothly was critical for his entire portfolio. As an accountant, Leslie should have understood the importance of this spot.

She understands all right, Nate, but no woman wants to be second in her man's life. Period.

He would make it up to her. Somehow.

When Nate entered the brightly lit office space, the manager, Denise, sighed with evident relief. He saw no customers.

"Thank God you're here," she said. "We've been slammed all day. This is only a lull between the storms."

Nate considered being swamped a boon to business; his staff often saw busyness as an inconvenience, despite the bonuses he paid when the store achieved specific sales targets—the difference between owning a business and working for one.

"Everything else good?" he asked.

"The printer's acting wonky. I haven't had time to try to fix it. Maybe you can work your magic."

"I'll take a look."

"Thanks for covering for me, boss. You're a gem. I've gotta go pick up my hubby now—he's been sitting on the side of the road waiting for me. Damn flat tire."

With that, she was gone, leaving him alone in the store.

Between assisting the occasional customer and other tasks, Nate examined the printer. He found the malfunction and repaired it using the owner's manual and a YouTube video. Learning to diagnose and fix his equipment came in handy; having to call and wait on repair techs meant out-of-service machinery couldn't generate income, and these days, the corporate office was pushing the stores to bring in more print job revenue. Merely handling packages wasn't enough anymore.

However, the job candidate never arrived for the two o'clock interview and didn't text or call. Getting ghosted by prospective hires was a frequent issue these days, too.

He had a couple of backup candidates he could call in. He hoped they would still be interested in the job, but there was a reason why he considered them "backups" in the first place.

Leslie texted him later that afternoon and asked him to pick up a handful of items from Publix before he came home. After locking the shop at six thirty, he strolled down the broad paved walkway to the supermarket.

He picked up a rotisserie chicken, a bottle of chardonnay, and a head of romaine lettuce inside the store, tossing the items into a handbasket. At checkout, he opted for a line staffed by an actual human being instead of using the self-checkout line. He understood the economics of encouraging customers to serve themselves, but it irked him nonetheless.

The cashier was a slender, forty-something Black man with a wooly salt-and-pepper Afro and a goatee that needed grooming. A faded scar curved along his jaw. He wore a tattered black fleece jacket over his uniform that concealed his name tag.

"How's it going?" Nate asked as he placed items on the conveyor belt.

The guy didn't respond or look at Nate, but when he scanned the bottle of wine, he mumbled, "Lemme see your ID," in a gravelly voice.

Nate had his driver's license ready. He handed it to the cashier.

The man gripped it with thick, calloused hands—hands built for construction, not scanning groceries. He studied the ID with unusual intensity, his dark gaze drilling into the plastic and then into Nate, as if he were a TSA agent who might recognize Nate's name from the no-fly list.

"I'm innocent." Nate chuckled. "But I've dropped a few pounds since I took the photo."

Without a word or a glance, the cashier returned his license and rang up the items.

Weird, Nate thought. After paying with a debit card, he grabbed his bags and went outside.

As he neared his truck, a man called out behind him.

"Hey, Nathan Noble! Wait up!"

Nate turned to see the same grumpy cashier hurrying across the parking lot. The guy shambled forward with a slight limp, favoring his right leg. Knee injury?

"Yeah?" Nate asked. "Did I forget something?"

"Do you remember me?" The guy smiled, revealing a chipped front tooth.

"Umm, no. Should I?"

"Bike rides and video games, Nathan. Remember? Thirty years ago, was it?"

Nate searched the man's deep-set brown eyes and his scarred face. He didn't recognize him, but did he say it had been thirty years? Nate had been twelve. Bike rides? Video games?

Could it be . . .

"Marvin?" Nate asked.

"Yeah! I'm Marvin Waters, man! Damn, it's good to see you, brother!"

2

———

Nate hadn't seen or spoken to Marvin Waters since he was twelve years old, not since that fateful day when he brought Marvin's bicycle back to his house and heard the blood-curdling scream . . .

He'd sealed those old memories and shoved them deep into the back corner of his mind. Some painful recollections had an almost supernatural power to wreck your spirit, and Nate had learned to keep a lid on them lest he spend his days in a perpetual state of misery and regret.

But with Marvin standing only five feet away on this cool January evening, everything poured back into Nate's thoughts. Nate shuddered, and emotion constricted his throat.

Could it really be Marvin Waters? After all these years?

"Marvin . . . man, I didn't recognize you," Nate said. His tongue felt thick; tears threatened to spill out of him. "I tried looking you up . . . I never knew what happened to you . . . after, well, you know . . ."

A shadow crossed Marvin's face. "Yeah. We lost touch. We were just kids."

"Wow, this is something else." Nate shook his head, a laugh

escaping him. "Marvin Waters! How've you been? Where've you been?"

"I never moved away. I've rolled around wherever work takes me. Sort of a nomadic life, I guess."

But you were always so bright, Nate almost said. Marvin had excelled in school. How had he ended up bouncing between low-paying jobs? When they were kids, a college scholarship and a successful career seemed guaranteed for Marvin.

Stop judging, man. All honest work is honorable. And remember what happened to Marvin—and what he did . . .

"Do you live in the area?" Nate asked. "I'm in Lawrenceville."

"I usually stay with my sister. In Norcross. Can you walk with me for a minute, bro?"

"Sure. One sec."

Nate placed his grocery bags inside his truck and walked across the parking lot alongside Marvin, who plodded ahead with his limp. It felt surreal to see his old childhood friend in the flesh again. He had often wondered about what had happened to Marvin—but he'd never imagined he would run into him like this.

Life was unpredictable, sometimes.

Marvin approached an ancient blue Oldsmobile Cutlass Supreme dating from the late 1980s. Rust spotted the vehicle, and grime coated it like a second skin.

Nate saw a heap of miscellaneous items through the dusty rear windshield: clothes, shoes, boxes, crumpled fast food bags, and other junk. Marvin claimed to be staying with his sister, but Nate questioned if he was living in the car sometimes, too.

No, he can't be living in his damn car. No way.

But with the crazy cost of living these days, with escalating rents and soaring real estate values? A whole class of folks had turned normal-size vehicles into mobile apartments. It was an unfortunate reality of modern times.

Marvin pulled open the driver's door. It shrieked like a wounded animal. Marvin reached inside, rummaged, and retrieved a pack of Kool cigarettes.

"You smoke now?" Nate asked, then regretted the question. They weren't twelve anymore.

"I wish I didn't." Marvin leaned against the door, shook out a cigarette, and lit it with a Bic lighter. He inhaled, closed his eyes as if in rapture, and exhaled a thin column of smoke. Satisfaction spread across his face. "Damn. I needed a quick hit. My boss is a straight asshole, bro. He's got me on the register dealing with these trifling-ass folks today, and he knows I hate dealing with those knuckleheads."

"Customers can be demanding," Nate said. "I get it. I see it every day at my job, too."

"Dumbass customers." Marvin sneered, glanced at Nate's jacket with the corporate logo, and gestured with his cigarette. "Hey, do you work in that UPS Store across the way?"

"That's right."

"How do they treat you there?"

Nate hesitated to reveal that he owned the store. Given Marvin's work situation, it might sound like bragging.

"I love it," Nate said. "Every day's an adventure, man."

"Is that so?" Marvin took another long drag. "How's family life, Nathan? Are your folks doing well?"

"Mom is great. Retired and living the dream." He paused. "You know my father was a nonfactor."

"That's right," Marvin said, nodding and puffing.

"How about your mom?" Nate asked.

"Are you married with kids, living in the 'burbs behind a white picket fence?"

Nate wondered why Marvin avoided his question about his mother.

"Divorced, no children," Nate said. "Getting ready for marriage number two in May. How about you?"

"I dodged those bullets."

"Lucky you."

Marvin exhaled a raft of smoke. "Weird how we run into each other like this, isn't it, Nathan? Work neighbors and all. Life's strange, huh? Is it fate?"

"Why did you put my ID under the microscope when I checked out? Did you know it was me?"

"I knew your name was familiar, but it didn't click until you walked out. I couldn't let you drive off without being sure."

"I didn't recognize you at all, man," Nate said with a chuckle. "I guess I look a lot different, too. Thirty years, dude. Father Time is no joke, huh?"

Marvin started to say something else when his phone buzzed. Glancing from the screen to the supermarket, his face darkening, he pushed away from the car.

"I wish we could hang out and reminisce, but I'm on the clock and not exactly the boss's favorite employee," Marvin said. He flicked his cigarette to the blacktop and ground it out with his work shoe. "I need to get back on that shitty register. Can I get your number, Nathan? We should connect soon." He grinned. "Hey, we can go for a bike ride, for old-time's sake."

Marvin laughed, and Nate joined in.

But to Nate, their laughter sounded bittersweet.

"I ran into an old friend today," Nate told Leslie as they settled down for dinner. "I don't think I ever told you about Marvin Waters, probably because of what happened when we were kids."

They sat at the round kitchen table, plates piled high with a chicken Cobb salad Leslie had tossed together from the items he'd picked up from the grocery store. As Leslie often said, she loved to cook but had no issues taking shortcuts.

She sipped her chardonnay, her gaze pensive. When Nate arrived home, her jaw clenched at seeing him; clearly, she was still annoyed because he'd skipped the cake tasting. He'd brought her favorite wine as a peace offering and apologized again for leaving early, but experience taught him it could take days to regain her favor. She was slow to anger but could be equally slow to forgive.

But his need to share his encounter with Marvin bubbled inside him like a shaken soda can.

"Marvin Waters?" Leslie's dark brows knitted. "No, you've never mentioned him. What happened back then?"

"He killed his stepfather."

Leslie's fork clattered against the plate as it slipped from her fingers. She gaped at him.

"He murdered his stepfather?"

"Thirty years ago. We were twelve, and Marvin's stepdad was abusive as hell. I saw cigarette burns on Marvin's back once. The kid lived in constant fear of that guy."

Horror etched Leslie's face. "Are you serious?"

"Marvin never said it outright, but I think the guy beat his mother, too. Until Marvin snapped."

Leslie's knuckles whitened as she gripped her glass. "Go on."

Nate recounted that April day: their bike ride, Mr. Waters' violent arrival, the forced departure. He described taking Marvin's abandoned bicycle to their house, discovering the open front door, hearing the chilling scream . . .

"I pushed the door open," Nate said. The old memory, vivid as ever, still raised goose bumps on his arms. "His mom was screaming. Marvin's stepdad was sprawled in the hallway, blood gushing from his throat. Marvin was holding a bloody butcher's knife."

Leslie's hand flew to her mouth. "You *saw* that?"

"That image is seared into my brain. I wish I could *unsee* it."

Leslie gulped her wine, staring at him with shock and amazement.

Nate's mouth felt like sandpaper. Talking about that day hit harder than silent mental replays. He pushed aside his wine for a glass of ice water and took a long swallow.

"Both of you, only twelve," Leslie whispered. "Jesus. That's horrifying."

"I had nightmares for months. Crazy dreams where *I* was the one with the knife."

He kept his theories about those dreams to himself, uncertain how to explain without Leslie drawing unsettling conclusions about his past choices. Yet the urge to unburden himself gnawed at him.

"I'm so sorry, babe." Leslie's fingers brushed his arm.

"That was the last time I saw Marvin," Nate said. "Until today, after I closed the store. He works at Publix in the same shopping center. Can you believe it?"

"Did he go to prison? He was twelve and abused, like you said."

"Mom said he was sent away. He probably did juvenile detention for sure, but I don't know for how long. I never learned about any details. I mean, I was a witness, right? But no one ever called me in to testify. Marvin just vanished into thin air." Nate snapped his fingers, the sound sharp in the kitchen.

"What about his family?" Leslie asked.

"His mom and sister disappeared, too. Mom heard through the grapevine that they'd relocated." Nate inhaled. "I've googled Marvin's name a few times over the years, but never found a thing."

"How sad."

"Seeing him today was great, but he's not doing well." Nate stirred salad around his plate with his fork. "He looks twenty years older than he is, and he's struggling with work, driving some rusty old car full of junk."

"A criminal record is like a scarlet letter, you know," Leslie said. "God only knows what happened to him since then."

"Marvin was brilliant when he was a kid. Super shy, but so smart. It's not fair what happened. I feel . . . responsible."

Leslie's eyebrows shot up. "Why?"

"I've never told anyone this." Nate averted his gaze, weighing his words. "The day his stepdad exploded? I'd slipped a letter under the school principal's door."

"A letter?" Leslie's glass hovered at her lips.

"It was an anonymous note accusing his stepdad of abuse and asking the school to investigate. No one was helping them, Les. This guy terrorized his family. My mother knew how bad it was but wouldn't get involved. Marvin was my best friend, and everyone ignored it." Nate's hands grasped at the air. "I had to do *something*, say something."

Leslie fell silent, her gaze downcast. Was she judging him, too? He wondered if he shouldn't have told her.

But he kept on.

"What if someone from the school called Mr. Waters at work?" Nate said. "What if that's why he went off on Marvin later? I've always felt responsible for that whole chain of events."

"You were only twelve, babe," Leslie said.

"I know, but—"

"If his stepdad were that awful, your friend probably would have snapped eventually," she said. "He was a victim, defending himself and his mother from a monster."

"I had good intentions." Nate pushed away from the table, his appetite gone. "It's not fair his life derailed because of me."

"It wasn't your fault." Leslie rose and approached him. "Let it go, okay?"

"It's not that easy, Les. I wish it were, but it's not."

"You're too hard on yourself. Will you ever learn to give yourself a break?"

Leslie pulled him into an embrace and held him close. He loved the feel of her against him, but it couldn't dissolve the guilt percolating in his chest like acid reflux. Seeing Marvin had torn the lid off those old feelings he had kept locked away; they wouldn't disappear now because of a few sympathetic words and a warm hug.

But connecting with Marvin again might offer him a chance to make amends. To do something good. To do something meaningful that might, in a small way, make up for the terrible turn his friend's life had taken.

But what could he do?

4

———

Two days later, Nate spotted Marvin outside the UPS Store in Norcross. Marvin paced the sidewalk, a halo of cigarette smoke following him. He peered through the store windows every few seconds, eyes darting, before resuming his restless walk.

Memories flooded Nate's mind. Back in the day, Marvin would come over to his house, knock, and then stand silent as a mannequin when Nate's mom answered the door, too shy to speak. Nate hadn't been able to tell his mother yet about reconnecting with Marvin. His mom was cruising the Caribbean with a group of girlfriends, living the retiree's dream on a well-earned pension, and was due back that weekend.

Why was Marvin there?

Nate worked the store alone; one of his associate clerks was absent (again) due to illness. Friday's usual bustle kept him on his toes. After serving the final customer, Nate stepped outside.

Marvin wasn't wearing his grocery store uniform. He wore a faded black fleece jacket, a T-shirt, and rumpled jeans. His Chuck Taylors were smudged with grime.

A five o'clock shadow peppered Marvin's cheeks, stubble flecked with gray. His eyes were bloodshot as if he hadn't slept in days.

Did Marvin ever get a decent night's sleep? Nate couldn't imagine how taking someone's life, even in self-defense, could burden your conscience.

"Hey, I planned to hit you up this weekend." Nate gestured toward the store. "This place keeps me jumping nonstop."

Marvin flicked his cigarette to the ground and crushed it under his sneaker. He ran his fingers through his Afro, avoiding Nate's gaze, his attention fixed on the parking lot.

His silence reminded Nate of the young Marvin. Marvin would often pause, weighing his words as if fearing a misstep. Nate sensed that the guy was nervous about something.

Nate already had decided to give Marvin money if he asked, with no strings attached. While guilt colored this decision, he was comfortable with it. He had to do *something*.

Marvin cleared his throat and inclined his head toward the UPS Store. "How's work today, Nathan? Knucklehead customers giving you shit?"

"Busy but manageable. Another employee called in sick."

"They could be sick, not lying about it." Marvin lifted his chin in a challenge. "Or there could be a toxic work environment here."

Nate's gut clenched. "The work environment is fine, trust me. It's hard to find reliable help these days."

"Whoa. You sound like management, Nathan."

"And you sound like you're job hunting, Marvin. What's up?"

Marvin's gaze drifted to the nearby Publix, his face tightening like a fist.

"I could be." Marvin shoved his hands into his pockets and rocked on his heels. "A rolling stone gathers no moss, Mama used to say."

Marvin's use of the past tense struck Nate. A rock settled in his chest.

"Come on." Nate pushed open the store door. "Let's chat inside."

5

Inside, Nate moved behind the counter. Marvin stood in the shop's center, mouth agape.

"You manage this place?" Marvin asked. "I've never been in one. Never had anything to ship or needed to rent a mailbox."

"I own it," Nate said, and he couldn't keep the pride out of his voice.

Marvin turned. "You own it?"

"It's a franchise. I'm a UPS franchisee with certain contractual obligations, but I oversee all operations. I have two other stores in Gwinnett."

"*Three* stores, Nathan?"

"Yup."

"Well, shit. Life's been peachy keen for one of us." Marvin plucked a business card from the counter tray. "There it is. 'Nathan Noble, franchisee, operator.' Good for you."

"Look, I didn't get to this point overnight. It's been a long, hard road to get this far."

Marvin's eyes darkened. "I don't need you to lecture me about hard roads."

"Right." Nate pulled his hand down his face. "I wasn't lecturing. I've worked hard, but I had lucky breaks and mentors along the way. No one succeeds alone, ever. Anyone who claims to be self-made is full of shit."

"I'm proud of you. You're out here repping our old hood like a boss."

"Thanks, man."

Marvin surveyed the store, examining displays and equipment.

I'm going to offer him a job, Nate thought. The idea had hatched in his mind last night, and he'd intended to test the waters when he called Marvin to set up a meeting. Marvin showing up at the store today, obviously fishing for a new job, gave him a chance to move forward with his plan.

Naturally, Leslie thought it was a bad idea. *Business and friends don't mix*, she'd advised. But Nate believed that offering Marvin a job —not a handout—was the most helpful way for Nate to lend a hand to his old friend. Folks hired friends and family all the time; nepotism was the lifeblood of many a company. Why couldn't he do the same thing?

You don't know how he's changed in the past thirty years, Leslie had pointed out. *He's not the innocent kid you remember.*

Sometimes, all anyone needs is for someone to reach out, Nate had fired back. *I wouldn't be where I am today if others hadn't reached out and pulled me along the path.*

Ultimately, Leslie agreed with him, in principle, but warned him to be cautious. Nate had already made up his mind.

"I have an associate clerk role that I've struggled to fill," Nate said. "Are you interested?"

"Associate clerk?" Marvin glanced at Nate over his shoulder. "What's the starting pay?"

Nate opened a drawer and retrieved an employment application. He slid it across the counter and gestured to a jar holding several ballpoint ink pens.

Approaching the counter, Marvin looked at the form but didn't pick it up.

"It starts at eighteen dollars an hour," Nate said.

"But you would pay me more than some unknown Negro off the street. Considering how far we go back, I'd expect you to sweeten the deal." He smiled. "Years of bike rides and video gaming ought to count for something, brother."

Nate hadn't expected that response, but he said, "It's negotiable. Depending on your qualifications."

The door opened. Several customers entered the store in quick succession, each of them bearing packages of various dimensions.

Without asking permission, Marvin came behind the counter. Nate frowned, confused, but didn't want to cause a scene in front of customers—and then he sensed what Marvin was about to do.

Speaking little, Marvin accepted each package, some of which appeared quite heavy, and placed them on the scale; Nate processed the orders, and Marvin carried the packages to an area farther in the back office for carrier pickup.

Working in tandem, they efficiently serviced each customer until the last shipment had been completed, and they were once more the only two people inside. Marvin returned to the other side of the counter.

"You didn't need to pitch in, but thank you," Nate said.

"You need a reliable pair of hands and a strong back. I've got both. That should be qualification enough for a more generous paycheck, man."

Nate couldn't tell if Marvin was serious; this was not the twelve-year-old Marvin he remembered. That shy, bright kid, quick to smile, slow to ever disagree or debate, had faded into the past.

"Fair enough." Nate tapped the job application. "I can do twenty dollars an hour. Cool?"

Marvin regarded the form as if it might cut him like a blade. "Is this paperwork necessary?"

"I'm bound to UPS corporate by those obligations I mentioned before. I can't hire someone off the books."

"The system is no friend of ours, Nathan."

"The system?"

Marvin cocked his head, studying Nate.

"Did you go to college?" Marvin asked.

"I graduated from Clark Atlanta. Mighty proud of it. I'd do it all over again."

"Of course." Marvin made a *tsk-tsk* sound. "A college education prepares you for the system, but not much else."

"What system?"

Marvin spread his arms as if to encompass the entire world. "Government. Society. Towing the line. Behaving as a good citizen, as it's known."

"Is behaving like a good citizen a bad thing?"

"We're all animals. At our core." Marvin took his index finger and traced that knife scar that curved along his face. "This is a mark from the *real world*."

Nate glanced toward the doorway, ensuring no customers were about to enter. He saw no one, but nevertheless lowered his voice.

"Listen, I know we haven't caught up on everything that has happened to us since we were kids," Nate said. "I realize a lot has changed."

Something unfurled in Marvin's eyes, for the briefest of moments. It recalled that time Marvin's stepfather had cut them off in the road with his car, and Marvin had tilted back his head, opened his mouth, and unleashed a scream that echoed in Nate's nightmares for years.

Then it was gone, and Nate wondered if he had imagined it.

"I live in the present," Marvin said. "What would be the point of rehashing the past three decades? You would probably feel guilty, and talking about my life would only piss me off. There must be a reason we ran into each other a couple of days ago, and I doubt it's so we can stew over past regrets and bad choices, you know?"

This had to be one of the strangest conversations Nate had ever had with anyone, but Marvin had always been a bit eccentric. Although Nate wasn't sure he agreed with his opinions about "the system," they didn't need to agree on everything for Marvin to work at the store.

"I'm glad we reconnected," Nate said. "The job is yours if you want it."

Marvin reached for the application.

"I'll fill this out," he said. "I understand we're all stuck in the system and we've gotta play our parts."

"To be clear, it's a part-time position, Marvin. We can discuss the details of the schedule, but you could work up to twenty-five hours a week if you want."

"That would be all right, yes, sir." Marvin plucked a pen from the jar and held it above the document; his gaze slid to Nate, a grin spreading across his face. "Are you going to run a background check on your boy? You know I'm no saint."

"I know what's up. Don't worry about it, but I need you to complete the paperwork for company records."

"When can I start?" Marvin started filling out the form. "You're seriously short-staffed."

A soft bell chimed. Another customer had come inside.

Nate took a deep breath. "You can start today."

6

"We're running late, babe," Leslie said. She rechecked her iPhone. "With the traffic I'm seeing on Google Maps, meeting the deejay at eleven thirty will be impossible. We've gotta drive to Decatur, remember?"

She and Nate were home on a Saturday morning, and Leslie again found herself in the uncomfortable position of herding Nate to a wedding-related appointment. He sat in his office at their house, tapping away on his laptop—working, as usual. He worked on his business even when he wasn't physically present in one of his stores.

Leslie admired his work ethic. No one could *ever* call Nate Noble a lazy bum. He put in longer hours than anyone she had ever seen and earned a fabulous income, much more than she made as an accountant. She understood that agreeing to marry a dedicated entrepreneur involved certain expectations and sacrifices, but when would he prioritize their wedding? Preparing for their Big Day apparently held the bottom spot on his To Do list.

She understood that he wasn't a fan of a splashy wedding and preferred a low-key affair, but she only asked him to take part. She wasn't demanding that he plan anything.

"I'm coming," Nate said. He leaned back in his chair, yawned, and stretched his arms above his head as if they had all the time in the world.

"We need to leave *now*," she said.

"I said, I'm coming, Les. Relax."

"I don't like being late for appointments. It makes me look disorganized."

"We can't have that, can we?" His voice dripped with sarcasm.

Leslie pulled in a deep breath. *Lord, this man*, she thought. *Please give me the strength.*

Slowly, as if he wanted to irritate her, Nate closed the computer, picked up a manilla folder off the desk, and shuffled behind her as she hurried to the three-car garage, clutching her wedding organizer against her side.

"I'll drive." He opened the door to his Chevy pickup. "Why don't you text Deejay Pookie and tell him we'll meet him at noon?"

"You know that's not his name." She laughed as she got in the truck.

"It's not?" He backed the vehicle out of the garage. "Deejay Boo Boo?"

"You're silly." She found the deejay in her contact list and zipped off a text.

Nate cruised out of their neighborhood. It was a subdivision of large two-story homes on spacious manicured lots, and many residents had young children. Nate had purchased the property before they'd met, but it fit the storybook life Leslie had imagined. Things were finally clicking into place for a prosperous future for them. They had a strong, caring relationship, stable careers, a lovely house, and, Lord willing, would someday (soon) have one or two healthy children to round out their lives. All they needed to do was stay focused on the essential things, and everything else would take care of itself.

To go to Decatur, he should have made a left out of the neighborhood; he cut to the right.

"Where are you going?" she asked.

"I need to stop by the Norcross shop to drop off some documents."

Leslie ground her teeth. "Seriously?"

"I'll take two minutes, Les. I'll pop into the store and be right out."

"I should have driven my car."

"Two minutes." He held up two fingers.

"As long as we get to our appointment by noon."

It took about ten minutes to reach the store in the shopping center. Nate parked in front of the location.

He started to get out and paused with his hand on the door.

"You should come in and meet Marvin," he said.

"You hired him already? I thought you were only thinking about it."

Nate's eyebrows twitched. She had learned to read his facial expressions. This one said, *Uh-oh, I should have told her.*

"Come in for a hot minute and say hello," he said.

He got out of the truck and slammed the door.

"Fine," she said under her breath. By following Nate, she could also ensure they didn't linger here too long and risk missing the rescheduled appointment.

Inside, Leslie found Nate chatting up Denise, one of the general managers she had met before, and a slender middle-aged Black man with an Afro so thick she initially thought it was a wig. A scar curved across his weathered face, his eyes nestled in dark hollows.

This was Nate's childhood friend? Leslie couldn't believe it. The guy looked several years older than Nate. But based on what Nate had shared with her, he'd probably lived a rough life, hadn't he? Stress could make anyone look older than their years.

"Marvin, I'd like you to meet my fiancée, Leslie." Nate touched her shoulder. "Leslie, this is my main man from back in the day, Marvin Waters."

Marvin came forward to meet her.

"It's nice to meet you, Marvin." Leslie offered her hand.

He let out a low whistle of approval. "Mmm. The pleasure is all mine, Miss Lady."

Marvin brushed aside her hand and stepped into her personal space, his arms open wide to embrace her. She didn't expect that, either, but she didn't resist.

His stubbled cheek pressed against her neck. He smelled of too much cologne and cigarettes.

As she was about to end the hug, one of his hands crept down onto her butt. He clenched her there. Jolted by surprise, Leslie snapped backward out of his arms.

"I look forward to spending time with you and my old best friend." Marvin smiled, displaying a fractured front tooth.

He meant to do that, Leslie thought, her cheeks burning. *It wasn't an accident.*

Leslie looked at Nate. Nate talked to Denise about the documents he'd brought in the folder and he hadn't noticed her interaction with his friend.

She was too civil to make a scene. Although she believed in her bones that the inappropriate touch was deliberate, part of her wanted to think it was an accident. *He's Nate's friend; he couldn't possibly have meant to squeeze my ass.*

Marvin smiled at her, but it looked like a leer. She felt her stomach knot. *Oh, he meant that booty-grab all right, girl.*

"We need to get going, Nate," Leslie said.

"Duty calls," Nate said to his staff.

As they exited the store, Leslie felt Marvin's gaze on her. She glanced over her shoulder, wondering if she was imagining things.

He winked at her.

7

———

As Nate drove away from the store, Leslie clutched her wedding organizer in her lap. She wasn't ready to let this Marvin business pass, not yet.

"Why didn't you tell me you'd already hired him?" she asked.

Nate glanced at her. She saw irritation flicker in his gaze, but he answered in an even tone: "Things moved fast, Les. I was going to tell you. Both of us have a lot going on these days."

"Are you going to order a background check on him?"

His gaze sharpened. "I already know what Marvin did."

"You know what he did thirty years ago. What's he been doing since then, huh?"

"I've hired my share of ex-cons, and they've done good work. Someone needs to give them an opportunity. I believe in second chances. Don't you?"

It was hard to debate what he told her, and under ordinary circumstances, she would have let it stand. But this felt different to her—call it the "he grabbed my ass" effect.

"You don't think it's important to know what he's been doing recently?" she asked.

"Marvin also had a job at Publix. Remember I told you about that? They run background checks."

"How long has he worked there?"

Nate gave her a full-on frown. "Why does it matter? I hired him. He *needs* work." He paused. "I needed to do this for him, okay?"

He squeezed my butt, Leslie nearly said. *Then he winked at me. Is that the kind of guy you want to work for you?*

But she kept her mouth shut. She didn't need to tell Nate what had happened, as if she were a child running to tell her dad about someone misbehaving. She had dealt with plenty of Marvins in her time, lecherous men who didn't respect boundaries and viewed women as objects created for their personal pleasure. Unfortunately, it was the reality of womanhood these days.

But if Mr. Marvin Waters dared to touch her again, she would check him so hard his head would spin. She didn't intend to give him the opportunity, either. She would do her best to avoid the guy.

Nevertheless, this background-screening matter weighed on her mind.

"You're the boss," Leslie said. "But I think knowing who you're dealing with is important. It could impact your business."

"I'm dealing with my old best friend who deserves a second chance."

"Hey, you're the HNIC. But don't say I didn't warn you later."

"Can we drop it, please? It's settled."

Nate squeezed the steering wheel and avoided looking at her. Shrugging, Leslie turned her attention to the wedding organizer.

They didn't exchange another word for the rest of the drive.

8

———

On Sunday afternoon, Nate visited his mother.

After retiring from the utility company where she had worked for forty years, Pamela Noble sold her Atlanta home. She moved to a two-bedroom townhouse in Smyrna. The new location brought her closer to Nate's younger sister, who lived in nearby Marietta with her husband and two school-age children.

Nate suspected his mother might have chosen a place nearer to him if he had settled down. She had often asked about his plans for a family, but after he turned forty and remained single and childless, those questions ceased—until recently.

"You didn't bring your wife?" Mom asked when she opened the front door and found Nate waiting outside.

"I don't have a *wife*, Mom. Not for another few months."

"Oh, okay." Mom chuckled; this was a frequent joke, and he took it in stride.

"Leslie's doing some wedding planning thing with her mother." Nate entered the house and shut the door behind him. "That's practically her part-time job these days."

"I'm truly looking forward to that wedding. From what I've heard so far, it will be stunning."

"I'm looking forward to it being over."

Mom's expression tightened. "Leslie's a good woman. She's doing this for both of you."

Count his mother as Team Leslie on the topic of the wedding.

"Anyway." Nate held up the air-conditioning filter he'd picked up from The Home Depot on his way over. "I'll install this. Is there anything else you need me to check?"

Nate had served as his mother's handyman for his entire adult life, visiting every few weeks to help with maintenance and basic repairs. He prioritized this responsibility despite his hectic work schedule. He would have been offended if his mom had hired a stranger for a job without first checking with him.

Maybe if his mother had ever married a man worth a damn, things would have turned out differently. But ever since he was a kid, it had been mostly just him, his mom, and his sister, and they'd needed to figure out how to navigate things.

"Can you check the main bathroom faucet?" Mom said. "There's been some slow leaking."

"Noted," Nate said. "Hey, guess who I ran into a few days ago? You won't believe it."

"Who?"

"Marvin Waters."

Mom's mouth dropped open. "*Marvin Waters?*"

"After thirty years, Mom! He was working at the Publix near my store in Norcross. I didn't recognize him—he looks a lot different now."

"My Lord." Mom put her hand to her mouth. "There's been so much tragedy in that family. How is he doing?"

"I'm trying to help him out." Nate shrugged. "What tragedy are you talking about? I mean, we know about the thing with his stepdad . . ."

Killing a man was hardly "a thing," but Nate had rarely felt comfortable expressing it any other way unless he needed to be explicit.

"Rachel—his mom—she passed away." Mom tapped her finger against her chin. "This was about ten years ago. She fell down some stairs."

"She fell down some stairs? In her own house?"

"That's what I heard. It's awful, isn't it? I went to the service. I may have the obituary around here somewhere." Mom shook her head. "I'm sorry. I thought I told you."

"I would've remembered. That's terrible for their family. Jesus."

Nate remembered how close Marvin had been to his mother when they were children. As a man with a strong relationship with his own mom, he couldn't imagine losing her in such a trivial accident. It would have crushed him.

"Did you boys exchange numbers?" Mom said. "You ought to bring him by sometime. I'd like to see him."

"I hired him for the Norcross store, Mom."

"Did you, now?" It was his mother's turn to look shocked again.

"He needed a job. I had an opening. Win-win in my book, despite what Leslie thinks."

"I see." Mom leaned against the hallway wall, her arms crossed over her slender chest. "You told Leslie what he did?"

"Yeah, she's fixated on me running a background check. But I already know all about Marvin's past." He gave his mother a level look. "We remember how he was."

"So shy that he'd hardly speak when coming to see you, I remember. I've always had a soft spot in my heart for that boy. He seemed like such a sweet kid."

"Marvin deserved better. I'm trying to do my part and lend a helping hand. Leslie doesn't understand that."

"She only wants to look out for you, sweetheart."

Nate glanced toward the staircase. "Let me get up there and pop in this filter."

"I'll try to dig up that obituary. I usually save them." Mom sighed again, and for an instant, she looked alarmingly frail. "Seems like these days, I get a new one every month from someone I know who passed on. That's part of getting old, huh?"

9

Nate replaced the air-conditioning filter in the attic and then checked out the bathroom faucet she had noted. The fixture required tightening; he kept a toolbox in his truck and used one of his wrenches to complete the job.

"I found Rachel's obituary," Mom said when he returned to the first floor. She offered him the funeral service program.

The obit's front page featured a color photograph of the decedent, Rachel Lily Waters. It was a profile picture taken from her youth: she was a stunning, dark-skinned woman with striking eyes and a dazzling smile.

"She was only fifty-five years old," Nate said as he studied the program. Sadness pressed on his shoulders. "I feel so bad for Marvin."

"There's something else I remember clearly now," Mom said. "Marvin wasn't there at the service."

Nate looked up from the obit. "He didn't attend his own mother's funeral?"

"His sister was there. She's drop-dead gorgeous, like her mom.

But no Marvin. Some of our old classmates and I talked about it, but no one knew where he was."

"He's listed here as a pallbearer." Nate skimmed the back page of the program again and put his finger on his friend's name. "That's damn strange."

"There must be a good reason. I sure wouldn't ask Marvin about it, though."

"It's most definitely an off-limits question." Nate passed the obituary back to his mother.

But the question echoed in Nate's thoughts after he left his mom's house. Why had Marvin missed his mother's funeral?

10

That Sunday afternoon, Leslie returned home from visiting her parents and spotted an old, rust-eaten Oldsmobile parked at the curb near their house.

The faded blue paint and dented fender stood out among the upscale neighborhood's gleaming late-model cars and manicured lawns. She filed the oddity away in her mind as she pulled her Honda Accord into the garage.

At her parents' house in Brookhaven, she and her mother had finalized the wedding invitation design. Nate, true to form, had opted out. "Just give me a tux, the time, and the place," he'd said.

A newlywed girlfriend assured Leslie that Nate's disinterest in planning was typical, but Leslie struggled to shake off the nagging fear that his detachment signaled reluctance. A decade ago, she had been planning a wedding with a man she believed was the love of her life. On the big day, her fiancé abandoned her at the altar.

The memory still stung.

She reminded herself that Nate surpassed her ex-fiancé in every way: he was mature, committed, honest, and loving. Yet those old anxieties followed her like a shadow.

She had switched on the shower when the doorbell chimed. She returned to the bedroom and checked the Ring app on her phone.

Instead of the expected delivery driver, the video revealed Nate's childhood friend and employee, Marvin Waters.

"What the hell does he want?" Leslie muttered to herself.

Marvin wore a black jacket over his UPS Store uniform. He carried a large, flat package wrapped in brown paper tucked underneath his arm.

Leslie's stomach clenched as she recalled their first meeting: his grabby hands, his leering wink. She hadn't told Nate, determined to handle it herself. Part of that sensible strategy meant she wouldn't answer the door for him when she was alone.

She texted Nate: *"Hey, Marvin's here. Are you expecting him?"*

No immediate response. Marvin rang again, then knocked.

Using the app's microphone, Leslie spoke through the Ring's doorbell speaker: "You're on camera, Marvin. Nate's not home."

Marvin pivoted to face the camera. "Hello there, Miss Lady. I come bearing gifts." He raised the package. "May I come in?"

"Sorry, I can't come to the door. Please leave it on the doorstep. I'll tell Nate."

"But it's for both of you." He shifted his weight, fidgeting. "Please, I need to give it to you."

"Just leave it. We'll get it later. Thanks."

"I only wanted to . . . to . . . show my gratitude." His voice dropped, his shoulders slumped. "I wanted to do a . . . a good thing."

Leslie's chest tightened. What was going on with this guy? His body language, tone, and word choice set off alarm bells. Every instinct screamed not to let him in.

He looked back at the camera. "Please?"

"I appreciate it, Marvin. But I can't let you in now. I've told Nate you're here."

Without a word, he set the package by the door and shambled away with a limp, disappearing from view.

Leslie felt a pang of regret. Had she been too harsh? Nate trusted this man enough to employ him. He'd only wanted to deliver a gift.

She knew she could be hard on people, slow to trust, quick to hold grudges. She was working on it in premarital counseling with her pastor.

But that first impression lingered: his groping hand, his leer. What kind of man acted like that when greeting his friend's fiancée— or any woman, for that matter?

Only a true creep.

She stepped to the bedroom window and peeked through a crack in the shutters. Marvin leaned against the side of the Oldsmobile. He lit a cigarette, took a long draw, and exhaled wisps of smoke.

Was he waiting for her to retrieve the package? Hoping curiosity would lure her out?

In the bathroom, water continued to gurgle down the shower drain. By then, she had probably wasted gallons of water.

Marvin kept smoking, propped against the car, facing their house. Leslie imagined him scanning each window, waiting her out as if they were engaged in a childhood staring contest.

Or she could be overreacting. Marvin could be only savoring a quick nicotine hit before his drive back to wherever he lived.

But the flesh at the nape of her neck prickled.

Go away, she willed him.

But Marvin remained posted against the car. Nate still hadn't replied to her text, either.

Wait as long you want, then, she thought. *You won't lure me outside with your little gift.*

She returned to the shower, staying under the spray longer than planned. Deep down, she realized she was trying to avoid the man who might still lurk outside.

Afterward, she toweled off, put on lotion, and changed into lounge pants and an old Essence Festival T-shirt. She avoided the window, leaving the blinds closed.

She set a timer on her phone for a thirty-minute nap. Although she usually dropped like a stone into sleep on those rare occasions when she could grab a power nap, slumber eluded her this time.

After she finally slipped into an uneasy doze, what woke her wasn't her alarm but the growl of an engine in desperate need of repair.

She rushed to the window just in time to see his car grumble away down the block.

Leslie checked her phone. She estimated Marvin had waited outside for at least *forty-five* minutes. Who did that?

With him gone at last, she retrieved the package—it weighed perhaps five pounds—and opened it in the kitchen. Inside, she found a framed pencil portrait of her and Nate, smiling side by side. The artwork stunned her with its skill and detail.

A handwritten inscription in the lower right corner read: *"I wish my friends a blessed future of love and happiness."*

It was signed: "Marvin Waters."

11

———

Nate studied the portrait on the kitchen counter. Although it was a black-and-white drawing, the intricate details seemed to leap off the page.

He turned to face Leslie. She had a sour look. It had become her default expression whenever the topic of Marvin arose.

"It's only a drawing of us, Les," he said. "A damn good one at that. I didn't realize that Marvin had artistic talents. It's probably something he kept secret when we were kids. He was so shy back then."

Nate noticed the muscles in Leslie's neck tensed visibly. He knew from experience that she was nowhere near accepting Marvin's unexpected visit.

When she had texted him earlier to tell him Marvin was at their house, it had taken him a while to respond as he'd been on a troubleshooting call with a software vendor's tech support. A few tense exchanges later, he'd relented and came back home. He had learned to gauge the temperature of her moods and sensed that she was near the boiling point.

"Did you give him our address?" she asked.

"Like I said when you texted me, he probably found it online. You can find anything online, and Marvin's always been sharp."

As soon as the statement left his mouth, Nate knew it fell short. But he couldn't understand why she was so worked up. His old friend had gifted them a piece of art, wanting to surprise them with an innocent show of gratitude. Why was this such a big deal? It wasn't as if some diabolical lunatic violating a restraining order had tracked them down.

"I don't like that he showed up unannounced," Leslie said, her manicured fingers drumming an agitated rhythm on the countertop. "He should've cleared it with you first."

"I was going to invite him over soon anyway, babe," Nate said, trying to keep his voice level. "I planned to talk to you about having him over for dinner."

Leslie's glare could've melted steel.

"What's your beef with Marvin?" Nate asked. "Are you still worried about that background check?"

"You're too trusting. I get it—you've got a big heart. But you don't know this guy anymore."

"We were best friends," Nate said.

Leslie threw up her hands. "Yeah, when you were kids! Thirty years ago!"

"He hasn't given me any reason to doubt him. If he does, I'll reassess. Give the brother a chance, Les. Damn."

Leslie spun away, the squeak of her shoes on the hardwood floor punctuating her frustration. She yanked open the dishwasher, and the clatter of dishes filled the air as she put them away.

Nate didn't bother telling her he had done detective work on Marvin. Before returning home, he had driven to the residential address Marvin had written on his employment application. He needed to see how and where his friend lived. He could've googled the address and viewed a photo on one of those real estate websites, but he wanted to check it out with his own eyes.

The address was a duplex in Norcross: a tidy house with

sunflower-yellow clapboard siding and green shutters. A couple of vehicles, neither belonging to Marvin, were parked in the asphalt driveway.

Nate remembered Marvin mentioning living with his sister sometimes, but he didn't see anyone outside the residence, and he wasn't yet so inquisitive that he would approach the house. He was only thankful that Marvin didn't seem to be living in his car like he had first thought.

His address verification would have failed to satisfy his fiancée. She wanted an entire background history on the poor guy; he could probably throw in a blood sample, credit report, drug test, and transcript from every school he'd ever attended. He could also include some character references for good measure.

Leslie didn't get it. At all.

"His life's been full of tragedy," Nate said. "Mom told me today that his mother died in a freak accident ten years back. She fell down some stairs."

"That's awful," Leslie said, not meeting his gaze. "I'm sorry to hear it."

"Mom went to the funeral," Nate said. "Marvin wasn't there, but his name was in the program." He pulled his hand down his face. "I can't imagine how he felt. They were close."

"He missed his own mother's funeral?" Leslie's voice dripped with disbelief.

"There must be an explanation."

"Short of being in the hospital or behind bars, I can't think of anything that'd keep me from my mother's funeral. Can you?"

"Did you have to bring up jail?"

"Or the *hospital*, I said. What other excuse is there for a son missing his mom's funeral?"

"It's not our business," Nate said.

"You brought it up." Leslie's gaze flicked toward him as she shut the dishwasher door.

"I'm not going to pry. It's only something that confuses me."

"What about his father? You've never mentioned his biological dad."

"Same story as me. Pops nowhere to be found." Nate shrugged. "That may be why we clicked as kids. Our dads abandoned both of us."

"That's a sad observation."

"Life is sad sometimes. That's why I try to do good, bring a little hope and positivity to everyone in need."

Leslie gave him what he interpreted as a skeptical look, and he felt a sudden and irrational wave of anger rise in him.

You can't expect her to understand, Nate. She grew up with both parents in the house, living a charmed life. Her family was like the damn Huxtables.

It was one of those gaps between them that occasionally surfaced. He couldn't blame Leslie for enjoying a stable two-parent household and all the benefits that came with it, but that wasn't his reality growing up. His mom had worked her tail off to raise two kids by herself, with no child support from anyone. When Mom finally got home after a long day at work, she was often too exhausted or stressed to attend to her children's every whim. Nate had learned independence at a young age—because he had no choice.

He was sympathetic to those born without advantages who strived to navigate life's ups and downs. He had been there and done that, and now that he had reached a certain level of success, he felt obligated to reach back and lend a hand. *To whom much is given, much is expected* was one of his guiding life principles.

Leslie had a good heart, but she could be too damn judgmental.

The kitchen fell silent, save for the soft murmuring of the refrigerator and the ticking wall clock, each second stretching the tension between them like a rubber band ready to snap.

"Now you're upset," Leslie said. "It's written all over your face."

"I have work to do." He pivoted to the refrigerator, opened the door, and grabbed a bottle of water.

"Can we talk about it?" she asked. "I don't understand why you're mad at me now."

"There's nothing left to say. You don't want Marvin around. I won't invite him over, then."

He picked up the portrait.

"I'll keep this in my office," he said.

"All right, fine, invite him over. I'll try to be civil, even though you need to know this guy better before you roll out the welcome mat."

"Having him over is sort of my plan to get to know him better."

"Right, but give me some advance notice, okay? I don't want to look up and be shocked to see him at the front door again."

12

The following Wednesday, Nate visited his Norcross store. Inside, Marvin worked alongside the manager, Denise, on a task beside the bank of rental mailboxes. It was midafternoon, when the business usually experienced lulls in customer traffic.

Nate asked Marvin if he could spare a few minutes to chat. He wanted to check in on his friend and invite him to dinner that weekend.

"I can take a break if it's okay with the boss lady here," Marvin said with a sidelong glance at Denise. Denise gave the thumbs-up.

Marvin joined Nate outside the store. It was unseasonably warm for January, with an overcast sky and a brisk breeze.

"Is everything okay, Nathan?" Marvin asked. "If this is about my visit to your crib again, I'm sorry. I didn't mean to upset your missus."

After last weekend's unexpected drop-in at Nate's house, Marvin had called Nate to apologize. Nate assured him everything was cool and told him to forget about it. Nate mentioned Marvin's apology to Leslie, hoping to put her at ease about the guy. She responded that

Marvin should never have been there in the first place—a typical Leslie response. The woman could hold a grudge forever.

"That's history, Marvin." Nate gestured ahead of them. "Come on, let's walk down to the Starbucks over there and grab a coffee."

The café was located past the Publix supermarket. Marvin hung back as Nate strolled ahead.

"Is everything okay?" Nate asked.

"My leg's bothering me today." Marvin winced. "It usually starts hurting before it rains."

Marvin's gaze touched the nearby Publix. Why did Nate suspect that Marvin was lying about his leg and was afraid to walk past the store? But why would Marvin lie about something like that? He'd told Nate that he had given his boss his two-week notice at the market, and it was all good.

"I can drive us over there, no worries," Nate said. "Wait here."

"Can we go somewhere else? If it's not too much trouble?"

"You don't like Starbucks?" Nate asked.

"They're a greedy multinational corporation, not deserving of your hard-earned dollars."

Do you realize that you work at a UPS franchise? Nate thought. *UPS being another massive company?*

But he remembered Marvin's earlier, quasi-philosophical remarks about "the system." Whatever the source of these beliefs, Marvin was a grown man, and Nate wouldn't persuade him to believe otherwise while standing outside on the sidewalk.

"Where do you want to go instead?" Nate asked.

"Is there somewhere independent, locally owned?"

"I know the perfect spot."

Nate went to his Chevy truck and pulled up to the walkway. With a muttered grunt and a wince of pain, Marvin clambered inside and shut the door.

"Nice ride, Nathan." Marvin traced his hand across the leather seat. "One of these days, I'd like to get a newer ride instead of pushing that old rust bucket."

"Thanks. Your Huffy was way newer than mine, man."

They laughed at the memory. In their moment of camaraderie, Nate thought about asking Marvin a few questions that had nagged at him. For example, *How did you get that gruesome scar across your face? Why did you miss your mom's funeral? Do you have nightmares sometimes about killing your stepdad?*

But he left those questions unspoken and drove to a coffee shop in a small strip mall across the road.

"I can let you off at the front here," Nate said.

"Before we go inside." Marvin paused with his hand on the door handle. "Can I tell you something in confidence?"

"Shoot."

"I don't want to get anyone in trouble, but this has weighed on me. I'm not someone who likes to snitch, either. Snitches get stitches, as they say."

Nate waited for him to continue. Where was this going?

"And I like Denise, personally." Marvin raised his hands. "Don't get me wrong. But you and I go back like rocking chairs. I'm obligated to share this tip."

"This is about Denise?" Nate straightened in his seat. "What's going on?"

"She's stealing from you, bro." Marvin's chapped lips tightened. "I've seen it. Twice." He held up two fingers.

"Denise Alvarez." Nate said the name slowly. "My store manager?"

"I saw her drop new printer ink cartridges into her purse," Marvin said in a hushed tone, even though they were in the privacy of Nate's truck. "She was trying to hide it, but I saw her do it."

"She can print whatever she wants right there at the store."

"That's what I thought, too, that it's an employee perk. But she could be stealing them to sell them. Those cartridges are expensive, bro."

"She's worked for me for three years," Nate said. He had encountered theft at his stores, but never from a manager-level employee.

And Denise? She was one of his most trusted workers. He found it hard to believe.

"Do you track inventory of those items?" Marvin asked. "I haven't been introduced to that aspect of the business yet, but—"

"I can check. But Denise manages inventory for Norcross."

"She may have tried to cover her tracks. She's a clever cookie, as Mama used to say."

"I'm stunned by this." Nate dragged his hand down his face. "Damn."

"I'm sorry to be the bearer of bad news, but we go way back, and I had to tell you." Marvin sighed. "That's what friends are for, right?"

13

———

Inside the busy café, they found a table in the back corner. Marvin had ordered plain black coffee, professing to be bewildered by the myriad beverage options—"I'm a simple brother; soy milk this and double shots of that mean nothing to me"—while Nate got a vanilla latte with oat milk.

Nate was reeling from Marvin's tip about Denise, but as soon as they settled at the table, Marvin shifted gears.

"Tell me all about the big wedding," Marvin said. He hunched over the table, hugging the paper cup in both hands. "You've got to be stoked to marry a fine, *fine* woman like that."

"I'm looking forward to marrying her, but extravagant weddings aren't my thing." Nate sipped his drink. "It's her day, though, and her family is footing the bill. I can't complain too much."

"How can a lifelong best friend get an invite?" Marvin snickered.

You're lucky Les agreed to have you come over for dinner this weekend, Nate thought. *There's no chance she's putting you on the guest list for her wedding.*

Also, what was this "lifelong best friend" remark all about? They hadn't seen each other in thirty years. But he assumed Marvin was joking.

"I'm not in charge of the guest list," Nate said. "I'm renting my tux and showing up to take the vows, man. This is my lady's Big Day."

"Of course." Marvin sipped his coffee. "Danielle keeps asking me about you. She's kind of sad that you're engaged."

"Your sister, Danielle?"

"All the good brothers are taken, that's what she keeps saying." Marvin shook his head. "She's stuck fending off the Pookies and Ray Rays."

"I haven't seen your sister since she was a little kid. I think she was five or six?"

Marvin bobbed his head. "She's thirty-six now. She's raising my nephew. He's nine. No father around to help out, unfortunately. I try to be there for him as his uncle, but you know how these things tend to play out, Nathan." Marvin shrugged. "It is what it is."

"I get it," Nate said. "You remember my mom raised me and my sister alone."

"But look at you now." Marvin smiled, but sadness tinged his eyes. "No one in my family ever gets lucky with anything, and no one ever has. It's like we're suffering from a generational curse or some shit."

Nate lowered his gaze to the table. He felt terrible for Marvin. And while Leslie thought his friend was a creep, the guy had endured a hardscrabble life on the margins of society, trying to eke out a living with a limited skill set in a fast-changing world. All she needed was to give him a chance.

Could he mentor Marvin in his business and eventually promote him to store manager? Had anyone ever given Marvin an opportunity like that?

This is why we reconnected, Nate thought. *I've got a chance to reach back and boost someone who only needs a chance. It's fate.*

"My boy is balling and shot calling," Marvin said. "Probably got investments and stocks and every damn thing. What do you think of Bitcoin, man?"

"I've dabbled in it," Nate said. "The folks who got into the crypto game early made the real money, though."

"Did you? You seem like one of those *Wall Street Journal* dudes."

"Just dabbling, man." Nate didn't like the turn in the discussion; talking about his investment portfolio felt like boasting. "Hey, do you have any plans this Saturday? Leslie and I would like to have you over for dinner. At our house."

Marvin responded with the broadest smile Nate had seen from him since they were kids.

"I'd be honored, Nathan." Marvin gave a slight bow.

"I'll text you the details, then." Nate cracked a smile. "You already know the address."

"Bro, I'm looking forward to this. All I do on weekends is work or hang out at the library. A dinner invitation is a special event for me." Marvin's eyes were glassy with tears, startling Nate. "Thank you."

But two days later, on Friday, Nate got a call from Denise. She sounded terrified.

"Boss, your friend's having a total meltdown! Can you get here now?"

14

———————

When Nate arrived at his Norcross store, he found a group of annoyed customers waiting outside. Denise had warned him that she had locked the door due to safety concerns, but she didn't explain what was happening inside with Marvin.

During his frantic drive to get there, Nate's memory returned to an incident from his and Marvin's youth. In sixth-grade gym class, their teacher had their group play dodgeball, a time-wasting activity the instructor directed them to pursue when there was nothing else for the class to do. But the kids plunged into the game with gusto, as boys often did when a winner-take-all contest was on the line. One of the kids, a notorious bully who stood a head taller than everyone else, heaved the fat rubber ball at an unaware Marvin, knocking him upside the head so savagely that Marvin nearly fell over. A comical, stupefied expression came over Marvin—and then fury flamed in his eyes. He snatched the ball off the floor and chased after the bully, fearless despite the other boy's intimidating stature, and hurled the ball at the kid's face, popping him in the nose.

A brief skirmish between the two kids broke out, but no blows landed, and neither boy got in trouble later. Nate had been astonished at Marvin's sudden rage. He didn't realize his shy friend had it in him to go off like that.

Nate had forgotten about that long-ago incident, but it was fresh in his mind when he arrived at the store around one o'clock in the afternoon.

Your friend's having a total meltdown.

"What the hell did you do, Marvin?" Nate whispered to himself as he hurried to the front door.

Customers milled outside, holding packages despite the "Closed" sign that Denise had hung on the front window. From outside, Nate couldn't see what was happening inside the store. Denise had dimmed the lights, too.

"I've gotta ship this package to my dad, sir," a guy said who Nate recognized as a regular customer. "Overnight."

"I'm sorry," Nate said. "We're temporarily closed, folks. Can you return in an hour, please? I'm very sorry for the inconvenience."

Grumbling, the people dispersed. Nate used his master key set to unlock the door, hustled inside, and engaged the lock again.

In the shadowed space, the first thing Nate saw was a jumbled pile of packages spread across the floor, at least a dozen of them, as if a windstorm had swept through.

What the hell?

The next thing he spotted was an overturned printer. The machine weighed at least a hundred pounds. Spilled papers surrounded it, as if the printer had vomited everything onto the carpet.

Nate found Denise huddled in the corner behind the counter, clutching her phone like a lifeline.

"Thank God you're here," she said in an anxious whisper.

"What's going on?" Nate automatically lowered his tone, too. "Where's Marvin?"

Denise cast an anxious glance toward the back of the store as if a grizzly bear had broken inside the storeroom. But the area was silent save for the ticking of the clock and Nate's drumming heartbeat.

"He got angry," she said.

Shit, Nate thought.

"What set him off?" he asked.

Denise flicked her dark hair away from her eyes. "He dropped a customer's package. It sounded like something broke inside it. The customer got upset. Your friend got *more* upset."

Nate remembered an offhand remark Marvin had made the day they reconnected: *dumbass customers*. It was obvious that Marvin wasn't cut out for a customer-facing role, but in Nate's eagerness to give him a job, he had put him in a position that demanded interacting with customers dozens of times daily.

"He had a total meltdown," Denise said. "Look around. He was screaming gibberish. It was terrifying. I had to get everyone out."

"Where is Marvin now?" Nate asked. "Is he in the back?"

"He's locked himself in the restroom. He won't talk to me."

"All right." Nate gathered himself. "Thanks for keeping your cool, Denise. You stay up here, okay? I'll go see him."

"Be careful, boss."

15

———

The small area reserved for employees was shadowed, too. The staff restroom stood across the hallway from the administrative office at the back of the store.

Nate knocked on the door.

"Marvin, it's Nate."

No answer.

A blood-chilling image seared Nate's mind: Marvin sprawled dead on the floor, a crimson gash in his neck, the victim of a self-inflicted knife wound—a wild juxtaposition of the horrifying scene Nate had walked in on at Marvin's house thirty years ago.

Nate shook off the gruesome thoughts and tried the door handle. Locked. He had the key but wanted Marvin to open up voluntarily.

Nate rapped his knuckles against the door again.

"Hey, man, can you open the door?" Nate asked. "Let's talk. No pressure."

Several seconds passed. Cold perspiration trickled down Nate's armpits. This situation was entirely outside his realm of experience. In his twenty-year work career since graduating college, he'd dealt with angry customers, frustrated employees, and irritated bosses in various capacities and roles. But this was something else. Marvin had a temper, sure; he had seen that when they were kids. But this felt like something beyond childhood outbursts and clashes with gym class bullies. He honestly didn't know what *other* issues Marvin might have developed in the past thirty years.

He killed a man, remember, Nate? When he was only a kid. That changes you forever. Of course he's struggling with trauma. You've no idea what triggered him, and might trigger him again.

"Talk to me, brother," Nate said, lips close to the door. "Friend to friend. I only want to be sure you're okay."

After a few seconds, Nate heard a shifting noise from the other side. Then, a click.

Marvin opened the door a couple of inches, releasing plumes of cigarette smoke. He peered out at Nathan. His eyes were bloodshot. Tears tracked down his cheeks.

"I don't want to get locked up again," Marvin said in a cracked voice. His breath was sour.

Why was he talking about getting locked up? Had someone threatened to call the police?

"You're not going to jail, Marvin. I only want to talk."

"Are you gonna fire me? I need to keep gas in the car. It gets so cold at night."

He sounded delirious, and Nate struggled to follow his words.

"Why don't you come out and let's talk?" Nate said. He retreated from the door. "It's cool, Marvin. It's only me."

With trembling fingers, Marvin put a glowing cigarette to his lips, took a long drag, and glowered at Nate through the screen of smoke.

"Come on out, man," Nate said. "It's all good. I'm your boy, remember?"

Marvin opened the door wider. After taking another drag on the cigarette, he flicked it onto the carpet outside the doorway and ground it out with his shoe, while Nate tried to hide his surprise that this man had just dropped a butt onto the floor inside his store.

"All right, Nathan," Marvin said. He ran his fingers through his thick hair. "All right. Marvin is cool now. Everything's copacetic."

"Why don't we go outside through the back door? It's nice and quiet back there. We can chill for a bit."

"Okay. That sounds good. You've always been so cool, Nathan. Did I ever tell you I wished you were my brother? I used to think about that all the time."

"So did I," Nate said, and it was the truth. He longed for a brother when he was a kid, and when he and Marvin became fast friends, he felt as if he had finally met a kindred spirit.

Yet here they were thirty years later, living lives that had diverged radically due to life-altering choices that could not be undone, and it saddened Nate.

Marvin shuffled behind him, dragging his leg, as Nate led him to the wide door at the rear of the store, the package-receiving area for delivery drivers. An electronic keypad beside the doorway required a password to unlock the door. While Marvin lingered beside him, his head hanging low, Nate punched in the code.

The keypad blinked green and beeped. Nate opened the door, cool air slipping inside and swirling around them. A large loading dock lay beyond the doorway.

Nate beckoned for Marvin to step outside, but Marvin paused. Straightening, he rubbed his hand across his eyes as if waking from a nap.

"I'm sorry for my behavior today, Nathan," he said. "I embarrassed myself and you, damaged your trust."

"I only want to be sure you're okay. Let's grab some fresh air and relax, all right?"

Marvin shuffled outside. Nate left the door open behind them as he followed.

They sat beside each other on the loading dock's ledge. From where they sat, they could see the back walls of the other businesses located in the shopping center: the grocery store on their left and a pizza franchise on the right. An eighteen-wheeler grumbled past, the trailer bearing the Publix logo.

Marvin lit another cigarette.

"When we were kids, I thought cigarettes were disgusting," Marvin said. He exhaled a cloud of smoke. "Now look at me. I'm a damn chain-smoker."

"We all have our vices. Hell, I'm a caffeine fiend. I drink coffee around the clock."

The Publix delivery truck inched into position behind the grocery store, the backup alarm beeping. They watched in silence, smoke twisting between them, their feet swinging free. They might have been boys again, just hanging out, if not for the weight of the past bearing down on them like an anvil.

"What happened today?" Nate finally asked.

"I'm not good at working with irate customers," Marvin said.

No shit, Nate thought, but he kept quiet and let his friend continue.

"The customer is *not* always right, Nathan. Whoever said that bullshit has never had to face a knucklehead customer. This lady today accused me of breaking her stuff, and that's a damn lie. She fumbled the package when she handed it to me, and that's why it hit the floor."

"Sometimes, it can be challenging dealing with people," Nate said. "It's the toughest part of the—"

Nate stopped speaking in mid-sentence. Marvin had straightened, his cigarette perched between his lips. His attention was riveted on the activity at the supermarket. His eyes sharpened to dangerous black points.

"Marvin?" Nate asked. "What's up, man?"

Marvin flicked his cigarette to the blacktop. Sliding off the loading dock and rising to his feet, he stubbed out the glowing ember with his shoe, but it was an absent gesture; he kept his attention locked on the grocery store, gaze fixed on the store employee who had opened the building's loading bay door to accept the truck's delivery, clipboard in hand.

Nate sensed danger looming, like smelling ozone before a storm. He pushed to his feet, too.

"Marvin, are you all right?" Nate said.

"That motherfucker." Marvin clenched his hands into fists.

"Who're you talking about? What's going on?"

Nate touched Marvin's shoulder to anchor him back to their conversation. But it had the opposite effect: Marvin strode across the pavement toward the supermarket's loading dock. His usual limp was barely noticeable as if whatever emotion was driving him rendered him unaware of his injury.

Nate tensed, unsure what to do. He called after his friend again.

"Marvin!" he shouted.

Marvin broke into a sprint. Nate snapped out of his paralysis and ran after him.

"You motherfucker!" Marvin screamed at the guy ahead of him.

The employee spun around, face draining of color. He stepped toward the doorway, but Marvin struck. With a roar, he launched himself at the man like a missile.

The two men crashed to the pavement in a violent tangle of limbs.

No, Nate thought as he raced to the melee. *No, no, no, no.*

Nate felt like he was running in slow motion, like this was a childhood nightmare in which his destination kept drifting farther away no matter how fast he pumped his legs. Marvin had pinned the guy underneath him. He threw a fist, and Nate heard the punch connect with the victim's face, a grisly thud of knuckles against soft flesh.

"Motherfucker!" Marvin shouted.

"Hey!" Nate seized one of Marvin's shoulders. Electric energy pulsed through Marvin's muscles like a lightning bolt had struck him, but Marvin ignored him. Nate wrapped both his arms around Marvin and dragged him away.

"Get off him, Marvin!"

His arms flailing, saliva foaming from his lips, Marvin thrashed out of Nate's grasp, and Nate tried to get ahold of him again. Grappling, they tumbled to the ground.

The impact against the concrete knocked the breath out of Nate's chest.

Marvin's fists flew. One punch connected with Nate's nose. Nate felt a sharp crack, then saw an explosion of white light behind his eyes.

"Oh, fuck . . . Nathan," Marvin breathed. "Sorry . . . fuck . . ."

Nate bled from both nostrils. His eyes swimming in tears, he saw Marvin clamber to his feet. Marvin spun around like a cornered animal seeking an escape route.

A security guard burst through the doorway at the back of the grocery store and aimed a Taser at Marvin.

"Freeze right there!" the guard barked.

Marvin raised his hands in surrender. He sank to his knees on the blacktop. His tearful gaze found Nate's, and Nate read his friend's lips.

"I'm sorry, man . . ."

Nate closed his eyes.

Soon, he heard the police siren.

16

———

Gently, Leslie pressed the ice pack against Nate's nose. Nate winced and reached to take the compress away from her.

"I've got it, babe, thanks," he said in a raspy voice.

Several hours had passed since the fight at the store. They were home. Nate was seated at the kitchen table while Leslie stood beside him, massaging his shoulder and fussing over him.

Back at the scene, a paramedic had examined Nate's injury and offered to take him to the hospital, but Nate declined. He'd suffered worse injuries playing high school football. He drove himself to a nearby urgent care clinic, got a bandage and a prescription for painkillers, and returned to reopen his store, much to Denise's horror; she had watched things unfold from the back door of their shop.

Despite all that, Nate struggled to process what had happened. His memory of the incident was a violent blur. The sight of police officers arresting a sobbing Marvin was the main thing he remembered.

First, Nate had been angry. Marvin could have destroyed that man if Nate hadn't grabbed him and hauled him off—and he got a busted nose for his trouble. What was the matter with Marvin for him to launch an unprovoked attack on the guy? Why the hell had he turned on Nate, too? Marvin had been thoroughly unbalanced, in a state of blind fury, and for a while, Nate thought Marvin deserved every punishment that the law brought down on him.

But a deep sense of guilt soon eclipsed Nate's anger. He didn't even understand *why* he felt guilty. Marvin was already in a volatile state after the argument with the customer in Nate's store, and when he saw his old boss from the supermarket, it clearly lit his fuse again. Marvin blindly slugging Nate was a case of Nate being in the wrong place at the wrong time.

Nate reasoned that maybe he felt guilty because, deep down, he knew Marvin suffered from unresolved trauma, and he had hired him anyway.

When Leslie arrived home, he told her everything. Predictably, she was upset that he hadn't called her sooner, but her concern for his welfare overcame her initial annoyance.

Marvin, on the other hand, had risen to public enemy number one in Leslie's book.

"I'm not going to say I warned you about him," Leslie said.

"But you just said it." Nate set the ice pack on the table. The pain in his nose had faded to a dull ache thanks to the cold treatment and the prescription-strength ibuprofen, but drawing air through his nostrils felt like inhaling tiny nails.

She pulled a chair toward him and eased into it. She rubbed his shoulder.

"You always want to see the best in everyone, babe," she said. "I love that about you, but at the end of the day, you need to face the truth."

"I know Marvin has issues. I'm not naive."

"He killed a man," she said gently. "Supposedly in self-defense."

"Supposedly?"

"You weren't there when he did it. You came on the scene after his stepdad was already bleeding out. And you don't know anything about whatever court case was held afterward."

Nate looked away from her. He didn't like the direction of this conversation.

But Leslie's words had dislodged an old memory, something he hadn't thought about in decades.

He and Marvin had been in the darkened den of Nate's house, sitting on the floor and playing Nintendo—some fighting game both of them loved, probably an entry in the *Street Fighter* series, where the contest was based on player-against-player battle. As the two of them controlled their players on the screen, pounding each other with a whirlwind of punches, chops, and kicks, Marvin suddenly whispered something in such a soft voice that Nate asked him to repeat it.

"I said, I wish I could kill him."

Nate was awestruck by the remark, and he didn't ask Marvin whom he was referring to—because he knew.

But Nate had said, this time in a whisper: *"Yeah. I know."*

Then, as suddenly as it had begun, the moment passed. They resumed playing the video game, and Marvin never brought it up again. But the conversation had stuck like a splinter in Nate's mind.

Thirty years later, he recalled it as lucidly as if it had occurred that morning.

"What is it?" Leslie asked, as perceptive as ever.

"His stepdad was abusive," Nate said. "Whatever Marvin might have done that day all comes back to how that asshole was beating the hell out of him. Marvin was terrified."

"No doubt he was. I'm not discounting the abuse. But you never got the full story."

Nate pushed away from the table. The abrupt movement sent a spell of dizziness whirling through him, and he had to lean against the kitchen island to keep from tipping over.

"What difference does it make now?" he asked. "What's done is done. That was a long time ago."

Leslie rose from her chair, too.

"He has a history of violence," she said.

He opened his mouth to fire back a disagreement, a defense of his friend, but couldn't summon any sensible words.

"A history of violence," she said again, in a somber tone. "He pummeled that man today, and he busted your nose when you tried to stop him."

"I know what he did. I was there, remember?"

"And *I know* you're carrying this guilt for some reason, and you want to help him get his life together. It's a noble thing to want to do."

"But?"

"But some people are beyond your help. You can't always be the hero."

"You make it sound like I have some kind of savior complex. What the hell?"

Leslie folded her slender arms across her chest, her brown-eyed gaze never leaving his face. She said nothing.

He looked away from her and opened the refrigerator, rooted for a bottle of nonalcoholic beer, pulled it out, and twisted off the cap.

Still not looking at her, he said, "I need to take responsibility for what I've done, the role I've played in things."

"Why are you still blaming yourself for a letter you wrote as a kid?"

"I'm not even talking about that." He took a deep swallow of the cold brew and placed it on the island's countertop. Staring at the stone surface, he shook his head. "I shouldn't have hired him. That's obvious now. He doesn't have the temperament to work in the store."

"I think I warned you about that, didn't I?"

He glared at her. "Don't gloat. I'm admitting I made a mistake, all right?"

She fell silent again.

"I should have given him some money," Nate said. "Not a loan, just money, for whatever. Then I wouldn't be in this mess."

"You don't owe him anything."

He picked up the beer. "To whom much is given, much is expected."

"Okay, babe." Leslie ran her fingers through her hair. "I swear, sometimes with you, I feel like I'm talking to a wall."

"Then stop talking about it."

It was her turn to glare at him.

"Cut him loose," she said. "Cut him loose and move on with your life. I won't stand here and say I'm fine with you trying to save this guy. He's toxic. He's dangerous. You being involved with him puts *both of us* in jeopardy."

"Well, he's in jail," Nate said. "We don't need to worry about it anymore."

"Really? Who do you think he'll ask to bail him out?"

"I left a message for his sister and told her what was happening. She can help him."

"But if he calls you, his successful business owner buddy? What're you gonna do?"

Nate didn't answer. He took a deep swallow of his beer, then another, and soon, he had emptied the bottle.

As he left the kitchen to toss the bottle into the recycling bin they kept in the garage, he saw Leslie leave the room, too, shaking her head with evident disgust.

When he returned to the kitchen, he heard his mobile phone ringing.

17

Around eight that evening, Nate arrived at the Gwinnett County Jail.

Darkness had already fallen, but the prison complex was impossible to miss. Towering spotlights surrounded the property at every angle, like sleepless sentinels: the jail was a multi-story, sprawling gray brick building covering dozens of acres. A tall metal fence topped with coiled barbed wire encircled the perimeter, its sharp edges glinting in the light.

After passing through a patrolled entry gate, Nate found parking in the visitors lot near the administrative office entrance. He switched off the engine and sat there, gazing at the prison through the windshield.

Once he went inside, there was no turning back.

His argument with Leslie still rang in his ears.

Of course Marvin spent his single phone call on you, she said. *He knows he can lay a guilt trip on you and get you to do whatever he wants. You're making a mistake, Nate. A serious mistake.*

But he doesn't have anyone else to turn to, Les! He's got no one else! I think his sister cut him loose—I can't reach her. I'll do this one, last favor for him and then I'm done.

Leslie responded with an epic eye roll.

Before leaving his house, Nate tried to contact Danielle, Marvin's sister, but again got no answer. He sent a text message, briefly summarizing the situation, but he was starting to wonder if Marvin had put the wrong phone number for her on his job application when he listed his emergency contact.

Or she doesn't care about her brother and doesn't want to be involved, Nate.

When Marvin had called Nate's cell phone earlier—a call Nate had been dreading but expecting—Marvin sounded deeply apologetic, ashamed even, his words coming in a rambling stream: *I'm not supposed to be here, Nathan. I'm sorry for what I did. I abused your trust—you took a chance on me and I blew it, and I'll make it up to you. I'm not that guy you saw today. I'm not, Nathan. Please believe me. Please believe me and help Marvin, your old friend. These animals in here, these rapists and thieves and murderers and addicts, these people are going to kill me if you don't help me get out. I'm not supposed to be here, Nathan. You know me, bro.*

The weight of the day had brought on a massive headache despite the painkillers Nate had swallowed earlier. He went to pinch his nose and remembered the bandage. When he walked into the prison, banged up like someone from *Fight Club*, he was going to look as if he belonged behind bars himself.

He climbed out of his truck and shuffled to the entrance.

Inside, a small vestibule led to a security checkpoint, which one had to pass through before entering the complex proper. A guard worked the post, more interested in her cell phone than assessing visitors. Nate emptied his pockets and proceeded through the scanner, retrieved his belongings on the other side, and followed the big sign pointing to the visitors lobby.

It was a short walk across faded gray tile floors to the next section. There, Nate saw two signs. One warned in fat red letters: "No Visits

Without An Appointment!" The other stated, "Visitor Sign-In," and directed him to a group of three kiosks equipped with electronic tablets; beyond that section lay a large, squarish chamber full of hard-looking plastic chairs and over a dozen people seated or pacing, most of them using their mobile phones. A prison administrator—just one —worked behind a counter protected with Plexiglas. She was chatting up someone behind her, in no hurry to process visitors.

Two kiosks had an "Out of Order" sign taped to the screen, leaving only one usable device. A line of eight or nine bleary-eyed people waited to use it.

I'm going to be here all night, Nate thought. He queued up for the kiosk.

The line moved with excruciating slowness. Nate passed the time looking at his phone; still no call or text from Marvin's sister. Another prospective visitor got in line behind him, bringing a fresh, summery fragrance. Nate glanced over his shoulder.

Whoa.

It was a gorgeous Black woman, her smooth complexion a rich, mellow brown. He guessed she was in her early thirties. She had long, lustrous braids framing a heart-shaped face. She wore a green bomber jacket, tight black jeans, and red leather boots.

Sensing his gaze, she looked up from her phone. Her smoldering sepia-brown eyes met his, and her full lips, adorned with reddish gloss, curved into a slight smile.

Nate realized he was staring. He coughed into his hand and turned away.

"Excuse me," she said, her voice low and melodic. "Are you Nathan Noble?"

Nate turned back to her. "Uh, yeah. I am."

"Wow." Her smile widened, revealing dimples and dazzlingly white teeth. "I'm Danielle. Marvin's sister."

Nate's mind reeled.

Doesn't it figure that Marvin's sister happens to be drop-dead gorgeous?

18

Danielle was still grinning at him. Nate smiled back, an automatic reaction, even though part of him felt that if Leslie stood nearby, she would give him a harsh rebuke.

Why are you looking at her like that, babe? Do you see something you like?

"I thought it might be you, because of your jacket," Danielle said. She had a sultry, throaty voice.

"Oh, that's right. UPS."

"Well, that and the nose." She gestured to her own nose. "In your message, you said something about a fight."

"Marvin hit me when I pulled him off the guy. He didn't mean to."

"Yeah, my brother and his unintended actions." She scowled, but she was so good-looking that even her frowns made her look beautiful. "I'm sorry I didn't get back to you earlier. I work two jobs, and I had to find a sitter for my son before I could make it over here."

"You're here now. I appreciate that."

"And *you're* here, which is amazing." Her grin widened as she shook her head. "My brother talks about you all the time since you guys reconnected. He hasn't had any friends, you know, so to run into you, someone from way back in the day . . . it's a blessing."

"It's funny how life works," he said. "But I can't honestly say that having Marvin work in my store was a good idea. I feel a little responsible for what's happened here."

"Don't say that." She shook her head, her lovely braids swaying. "You only tried to help, like everyone does. But no one can help my brother."

"What does that mean?"

As he waited for her to respond, he realized that the line had progressed and it was his turn to sign in. He punched in his information and checked the boxes for the purpose of his visit—"Post Bail for Inmate"—and the inmate information.

Typing in "Marvin Waters" as the inmate name failed to return a result.

Danielle moved beside him and peered at the screen. "He didn't tell you that he legally changed his name? Hmph, that figures."

"What's his new name?" Nate asked.

"Bediako Seidu. Going back to his African roots or whatever. You know he's always got his head in a book."

Danielle spelled the name for him and he typed it in, and this time, it found Marvin's record and he finished the check-in process. Then, he stepped aside so Danielle could do the same.

He waited for her to complete her entry on the screen, and then they settled onto chairs next to each other in the waiting area.

"Now, we wait," Nate said.

But he was acutely aware of Danielle's proximity to him. Her side profile—*those lips, those eyes*—captivated him, her fragrance blanketing him in a sweet haze. He swallowed hard.

Danielle unzipped her jacket and peeled it off her shoulders. She wore a tight red V-neck sweater that hugged her curves. Nate's throat tightened again.

Lord have mercy, she's built.

He couldn't remember the last time being in a woman's presence had affected him like this. Well, not quite true—meeting Leslie for the first time when she wandered into one of his UPS Stores had been like getting smashed by a barbell that fell out of the sky.

But Leslie's beauty was subtle. Danielle exuded the kind of stunning allure that made men swivel and gawk. Nate glanced around, noticing every man in the room stealing looks at her, some more discreet than others. She drew male attention like a magnet.

Why are you comparing this woman to your fiancée? What does it matter? You love Leslie and you're marrying her in five months.

Danielle's eyes sparkled as if she were privy to his thoughts.

"To get back to your question," she said, and he had forgotten what he had asked her to begin with, but she went on. "Marvin is going to do what Marvin wants to do. He's too smart for his own good. An educated fool. Just because you've read every book in the library doesn't mean you know how to make smart life choices, know what I mean?"

"He's got some anger management issues, that's for sure."

"Chile, who you tellin'?" Danielle said. "Do you know how many jobs he's gotten fired from in only the past three years?"

"More than one?" Nate said.

Danielle held up four fingers. He noted her fingers were slender, her nails perfectly manicured.

"Four jobs?" he asked.

It's about to be five, he thought, but he saw no point in sharing that little tidbit with her.

"He's had two restraining orders on him from people at those jobs, too," she said.

About to be three restraining orders, he thought, thinking about the grocery store manager Marvin assaulted that afternoon.

"He exploded earlier today," Nate said. "Totally lost it."

"It's only the tip of the iceberg, as the saying goes. I could tell you things about my brother that would blow your mind, honey." She glanced away for a beat, a faraway look in her eyes. "Some other time."

"His life is a train wreck. How long has this been going on?"

"His entire life? Well, ever since . . . you know what happened back then, right? Of course you do."

Nate nodded.

Shaking her head, Danielle sucked in her bottom lip. "I'm tired, Nate. Mama's gone—did he tell you that?"

"I heard she passed ten years ago. I'm sorry."

"It's only me now. We've always had a small family. I'm trying to raise my son to be a man, all by myself—my baby is my *number one* priority."

"What's your son's name?" Nate asked.

"Jaquon," Danielle said with evident pride. "He's nine. My little man. He's my focus, and I can't afford to keep getting entangled in my brother's mess. I don't have the money, the time, or the energy." She shifted toward Nate on the chair, giving him the full effect of her large, simmering eyes. "I only came here tonight because I knew you'd be here, and I wanted to tell you the truth about my brother."

"I'm going to post bail for him," Nate said. He made a cutoff gesture with both hands. "Then, I'm done. My fiancée is upset that I'm doing this much for him."

"She sounds like a smart lady. You should listen to her."

"You don't think I should post bail for your brother?"

"I'm not putting up a penny for him." She crossed her arms over her bosom and poked out her bottom lip.

"I already told him I would do it," Nate said. "I've gotta keep my word, and like I said, if it hadn't been for me, he wouldn't have been put in this situation. He was only at the store today because I hired him. I should have known better."

"You're a good man." She looked at him, a gentle smile flickering on the edges of her lips. "How long have you known your fiancée?"

"Three years. Why?"

"It's a shame our paths didn't cross three years ago."

The audacity of her comment caught him off guard. He laughed, but Danielle held his gaze, her lips still turned up in that soft smile. There was a challenge in her eyes—and perhaps a promise, too.

Warmth spread through his chest. But it was a dangerous feeling, and he knew it. It wasn't a sensation a man five months away from his wedding ought to be experiencing when he locked eyes with another woman.

Nate's phone vibrated, shattering the moment. It was a text message from the Gwinnett County Department of Corrections.

"I'm up," he said, rising from the chair and pivoting toward the counter.

"I'll be here," she said.

He felt Danielle's gaze on him as he crossed the room to post bail for his friend. Despite himself, her flattery gave him a thrill of excitement during what had otherwise been an awful day.

19

When Marvin finally emerged through the inmate processing doorway, looking disheveled in the same work clothes he had been wearing earlier, his bushy eyebrows knitted at seeing his sister standing beside Nate.

"I called you, Nathan, not her," Marvin said. "What is *she* doing here?"

"I left her a message and told her what's going on," Nate said. "I thought she needed to know."

"Nice to see you, too, Brother." Danielle rolled her eyes. "Don't worry, I didn't put up a dime for your bail. If it weren't for your friend here, your rusty butt would still be in there."

All right, I don't need these two making a scene while we're still in the prison, Nate thought, *and I don't want to be stuck in the middle of their family drama.*

"Why don't we get out of here, guys?" Nate said.

Marvin and Danielle followed him down the corridor to the exit, but kept bickering.

"Then you should have stayed home, Danny," Marvin said.

"I came to tell your friend all your business, since I know you won't," she shot back. "Are you going to reimburse him for the bail money?"

"I'll work that out with Nathan. Stay out of it."

"You owe me money, too. When are you paying me back?"

"Now is not the time, Danny. I'm tired and I'm hungry."

They left the building. Outside, the temperature had dropped several degrees since Nate had gotten there, and a bracing wind had arrived, too. Clouds of air puffed from their mouths.

"So," Nate said. "What now?"

"I left my car parked at your store," Marvin said.

Zipping up her jacket, Danielle made a *tsk-tsk* sound. "Sounds like you'd better get an Uber, brotherman."

"I can drive you there," Nate said. "It's no trouble."

"Thank you, my brother," Marvin said.

"Haven't you done enough for this fool?" Danielle cast an irritated glance at Marvin.

"It's on my way home anyway," Nate said. "Really, it's no problem."

"I've gotta get home to my son." She gave Nate a direct, intense look. "It was *very* nice meeting you, Nate."

"Same here, Danielle."

"Call me Danny, sweetie."

Nate raised his hand to give her a parting handshake, but she stepped close and opened her arms to pull him into an embrace. She squeezed him, pressing the length of her body against him. Her fragrance swirled around him in the wind, her silky braids rustling against his neck.

"You're a good man," she whispered, her minty breath warm against his ear. "Be careful with my brother."

She kissed his cheek, her lips soft on his skin, then slipped away, leaving Nate's heart pounding.

She didn't say goodbye to Marvin; she only rolled her eyes at him and then strutted to the parking lot, boots clicking across the pavement. Marvin looked as if he wanted to spit at her.

"Thanks again, Nathan. I owe you, big time."

"Let's get going," Nate said.

20

"I'm starvin' like Marvin, bro," Marvin said once they climbed into Nate's truck. He snickered at his joke.

"It's almost ten o'clock." Nate started the engine. "I could swing through a drive-through if that's okay."

"Beggars can't be choosers. Whatever's convenient along the way."

Nate navigated out of the prison parking lot.

"I'm not going to ask you how it was back in there," Nate said. "I'm sure you're glad to be out."

"You ain't never lied." Shaking his head, Marvin blew out a heavy breath. "Have you ever spent time in the joint?"

"My only brush with the law was a speeding ticket twenty-some years ago."

"Good for you—the system is no friend of ours," Marvin said. His voice had taken on a professorial tone, as if he were delivering a lecture. "Mass incarceration as it exists in this country is inhumane and corrupt. Do you realize that the American prison system generates billions of dollars in revenue each year, and those held in bondage receive little if any of the profits?"

"I've heard the stats," Nate said.

"It's the new legalized slavery. They're earning billions off the back of the unjustly incarcerated Black man."

"I've heard that, too," Nate said, in a neutral tone.

"We're trapped in the system, my brother." Marvin snorted as he looked behind them at the receding jail complex. "Pawns on the chessboard."

"All we can do is the best we can. I try to stay out of trouble."

"Trouble seems to find me. Like a shadow."

Nate grunted. Trouble hadn't *found* Marvin—he had kicked down its door and rushed inside. Marvin was damned lucky that despite his assault on the store manager and his prior record, Nate was able to post bail for his release so soon after the incident. The law wasn't always so lenient.

I could tell you things about my brother that would blow your mind…

Marvin swiveled toward Nate and studied him, squinting.

"What is it?" Nate asked.

"I suggest you forget whatever Danny told you about me," Marvin said. "They're lies and half-truths, mostly."

"She mentioned a couple of restraining orders against you."

Marvin waved his hand. "Like I said. Lies and half-truths."

"You've never had a restraining order on you?"

"Never." Marvin touched his chest. "I swear on my dear mother's grave."

"Why would Danielle say that, then?"

"She's a busybody, loves gossip and rumors. She's a typical woman, bro."

"A typical woman?" Nate gave him a pointed look. "Dude, I can see why you two don't get along." *And why you don't have a woman in your life right now*, Nate thought but didn't say.

Marvin flicked away his words with a dismissive gesture. For a few minutes, they traveled in silence.

Nate mulled over what Danielle had said about her brother. He believed her; any guy who assaulted someone unprovoked like he had was likely to have multiple charges and restraining orders on his record. Why was Marvin lying to Nate about it, even invoking his deceased mom? What kind of person did that?

He's toxic, Leslie had warned. *Cut him loose.*

But Nate had bailed him out, as promised, and it was settled: Marvin was free again. Leslie would never agree with what he had done. He understood her perspective, but she didn't understand— and probably never would—why he'd felt compelled to help Marvin one last time.

As a matter of fact, Nate wasn't sure he fully understood his own feelings on the matter. Was he helping Marvin out of some misguided sense of charity? Purely out of guilt? Marvin seemed like one of those perpetual screwups who had a knack for messing up his life, and at some point, you had to walk away and let him figure it out on his own.

But Nate had always struggled with turning his back on people, whether they deserved his assistance, or not. It seemed like his cross to bear in life.

"I must say, Nathan," Marvin said, "I'm looking forward to returning to work and repaying the money you put up for me this evening. I pay back all my debts. It may take me a while, but I'm good for it, believe that."

Here we go, Nate thought. He squeezed the steering wheel a little more tightly. He hadn't wanted to delve into the work discussion right then but didn't see a way to avoid it.

"About working at the store," Nate said. "I'm not sure that's a good fit for you right now, Marvin."

Marvin stared at him. "Come again?"

"It's a customer-facing job. Sometimes customers get upset and we have to deal with them. It's not the right role for you."

"I'm certain there's a back-office position that's better for me."

"The UPS Store is a retail business, on the front lines. There's no back-office position. I own the stores, and I work face-to-face with customers almost every single day."

"This sounds like you're firing me, man. Kick a brother when he's down, huh? Am I right?"

Nate looked at him. "I'll help you find something else."

Teeth bared, Marvin raised his right hand. He had a bandage on two of his knuckles, and Nate wondered if it was from him injuring his hand when he—inadvertently, supposedly—punched Nate in the face. Tension leaped like a live wire through Nate's arms.

If he punches me again . . .

Marvin lowered his hand into his lap.

"I want you to take some time, sleep on it," Marvin said. "We'll have this discussion later. In the meantime, I'll step back and let the dust settle. Is that good?"

I'm not going to change my mind tomorrow, or next week, or next month, or even next year, Nate thought. But he was too exhausted to argue the point further.

"Look, there's a Taco Bell up ahead," Nate said. "Cool?"

"Like I said, beggars can't be choosers."

21

———

I t was a short drive from the Taco Bell to the shopping center parking lot where Marvin had left his car. At that late hour, the area was mostly empty, and the storefronts—including Nate's UPS Store—were dark and shuttered.

Nate pulled the truck next to Marvin's Oldsmobile.

"Thank you for everything, bro." With the bag of food on his lap, Marvin offered his hand to Nate, and they shook.

"Take care of yourself, Marvin," he said.

"Can you hang out for a minute while I start the car? The old girl can be finicky in cold weather."

"No problem."

Marvin climbed out of the truck and eased into his car. Nate grabbed his phone and texted Leslie: "*Finally about to come home, see you soon,*" he wrote, concluding the message with a heart emoji. Leslie replied with a thumbs-up.

But Marvin seemed to be having car trouble. He exited the vehicle, shuffled to the front, and popped the hood.

This has seriously got to be the longest day of my life, Nate thought. He wanted to get home, toss back another ibuprofen, and crawl into bed.

Instead, he got out and joined Marvin in front of his car. Marvin hunched over the engine, condensation from his lips clouding his head.

"It's the battery," Marvin said. "I've been meaning to replace it. Can you give me a jump?"

"Do you have jumper cables?" Nate asked.

"Nope. Do you?"

Nate didn't understand why any sensible adult would drive a thirty-something-year-old car without keeping a set of booster cables handy, but as he was learning about his friend, planning ahead wasn't exactly his forte.

"Hang on." Nathan dug into the emergency roadside kit he kept stored in his truck's flatbed and grabbed cables.

They connected their respective vehicles' batteries and followed the correct steps, but the Oldsmobile failed to start. Nate exited his truck and joined Marvin again in front of his car.

A cold, steady rain had begun to fall, and the night's temperature felt as if it had neared the freezing point.

"It may not be the battery," Marvin said. He rooted under the hood like a blind man, touching random wires and components.

"We're not going to figure it out tonight, standing out here in the rain," Nate said. "Can I drop you off somewhere? Where are you staying?"

"I can manage." Marvin continued to trace his fingers over the engine compartment. "You've helped me enough today."

"You're going to sleep in your car?"

"I've got plenty of blankets and pillows. I'll be all right."

Nate stared at him, icy rain droplets trickling down his face.

"Get in the truck, Marvin. Please. I'm not leaving you here to sleep in your car when it's near freezing tonight. That's not an option."

"You're a good brother, the best."

They unhooked the booster cables and snapped shut the vehicle hoods. Nate waited in the truck while Marvin gathered his things from his car. He finally emerged with a gigantic, weathered duffel bag that he stowed near his feet as he buckled himself in the passenger seat.

"Where to?" Marvin asked. He tore into the bag from Taco Bell and unwrapped a taco, food spilling over his lap.

Usually, Nate didn't allow anyone to eat in his truck, but he let it go. They had more important matters to figure out.

"You tell me where to go," Nate said. "Is your sister an option? You said before that you crash with her."

Marvin devoured a taco. "Danny's plenty pissed at me tonight. You saw that yourself."

"Right."

"You've got a spacious crib, man. Are there any spare bedrooms?"

Nate laughed out loud at the absurdity of the suggestion. "Leslie would strangle me if I brought you home. That's no lie."

"Your woman sets the terms? In *your* house?" Marvin swallowed and packed more food into his mouth, his cheeks bulging.

"I've already taken a lot of heat from her because of my involvement with you. She didn't want me to post your bail."

"Women," Marvin said. "She doesn't understand how we go back like rocking chairs. Childhood best friends."

Nate felt his headache intensify. He didn't like how Marvin tried to manipulate him by using their old friendship.

"Staying at my house isn't an option, Marvin. Call your sister. Please."

Marvin slipped his phone out of his pocket. Nate expected him to make a call or send a text, but he showed Nate the screen.

It was a photo from one of those real estate websites, Zillow or whatever. A pic of Nate's home.

"You've got five bedrooms at your house," Marvin said. "But you can't spare one for your old best friend because you're letting some bitch tell you what to do. You've been cuckolded. *Man the fuck up.* It's your crib. You set the rules."

Nate gaped at him.

"First of all, don't call my fiancée a bitch, man. Ever. You're way out of line."

Marvin laughed at him and crammed another taco into his mouth, lettuce spilling from his lips.

"Second of all, why are you looking up my house?" Nate asked. "That's foul."

Marvin's laughter died down. "You're right. I apologize. I misspoke. When I'm exhausted and stressed, I make inconsiderate remarks. I'm sorry."

Nate waved off his words. "I'm done. Call your sister."

But Marvin opened his door and grabbed his duffel bag off the floor.

"What the hell are you doing?" Nate asked.

"Run home to your woman," Marvin said.

Marvin saluted Nate, climbed out of the truck, and slammed the door.

22

As Nate watched in disbelief from the warmth of his truck, Marvin clambered back inside his car.

This fool is actually going to stay here, Nate thought. *He's going to sleep in his car on a freezing night.*

But Marvin was a grown man. Nate couldn't *force* him to come with him; he couldn't make him do anything. If Marvin wanted to cocoon himself in blankets and hunker down in his car, wasn't that his choice?

"I can't believe this guy," Nate said out loud.

Nate drummed his fingers on the steering wheel. The rain hammered the night with greater ferocity, and wind screeched around the truck.

But hot air blew from the vents, wrapping Nate in a pleasant shroud. He looked at Marvin's car again. The downpour obscured his friend from view, but he had to be shivering in there.

I can't do it, Nate thought. *I can't just leave him here.*

He got out and knocked on Marvin's window. Marvin rolled down the glass a couple of inches, the window squeaking. Cigarette smoke drifted through the gap; the car's interior was so dark that Nate could barely see Marvin's face.

"Come on," Nate said. "I'll take you to a motel."

23

———

"I apologize again for what I said earlier," Marvin said in a shaky voice. "I crossed the line with my comment about your fiancée, and I've no business looking up your house. Sorry."

Sitting in the passenger seat while Nate drove, Marvin hugged his tattered duffel bag against his chest like a toddler clutching a teddy bear. Tears streamed down his cheeks.

He looked pathetic. Nate could never have lived with himself if he had allowed this guy to spend the night in his car. As much as Leslie despised Marvin, Nate was confident that even she would have agreed with his decision to intervene.

"We've both had a long day," Nate said. "Forget it."

They rode together in silence, but it was a short trip to a budget motel. Nate veered into the parking lot.

"Motel 6?" Marvin said.

"Were you expecting the Four Seasons?"

"Nah, it's all good. I've slept in far worse places."

"Like your car." Nate parked near the building's front office.

"Worse than that. Have you ever seen those encampments

beneath highway underpasses around the city, people living in tents and boxes?"

"Seriously?" Nate said.

"I'm not proud of it." Marvin's voice quivered. "I know you expected better of me. Mama sure did."

Nate's hand trembled as he switched off the ignition. "Come on. Let's go get you a room."

Marvin followed him inside, lugging his gigantic duffel bag. At the front desk, Nate paid for a three-night stay.

"Add it to my debt to you," Marvin said. "I'll pay you back in full. I promise."

Despite Marvin's earnest words, Nate didn't expect Marvin to repay him. The guy had just confided that he'd occasionally been homeless, and he was still waging a war against poverty. Unless Marvin happened upon some unexpected windfall or completely turned his life around, Nate wasn't getting back anything from him, ever.

"There's no hurry," Nate said. "Whenever you have the funds is fine."

They shuffled back outside. Marvin's room was on the second floor. They stood beneath the front office awning, rain drumming on the roof.

"I need to get home." Nate yawned. "It's been a helluva day, huh?"

"I'm sorry for what I put you through," Marvin said.

Tears shining in his eyes, Marvin pulled Nate into a hug. Marvin smelled awful—a foul mixture of funky body odor and cigarettes—and Nate hoped the first thing Marvin did when he got in his room was enjoy a long shower.

"I'll check in with you soon," Nate said. "Take care of yourself, brother."

"What time is dinner tomorrow, Nathan?"

"Huh?" Nate stammered. "Dinner?"

"Earlier this week, you invited me to supper in your lovely home.

I've been looking forward to that meal, spending quality time with you and your beautiful fiancée. The idea gave me hope when I was locked up today."

Is he delusional? Or is he kidding? After all this, he still thinks we're having a dinner party?

But Marvin watched him, eyes gleaming. He looked as sincere as Nate had ever seen him.

He's serious as a heart attack.

"We'll need to reschedule," Nate said. "I'll get back to you."

Marvin dropped his duffel bag on the ground.

"I told you I was sorry, man," Marvin said in a low growl threaded with tension. "I meant it."

"I know you did, but look what happened today, man! Leslie won't be down with having you over at the house anytime soon."

"You let that bitch run you, brother."

"I told you, man, don't call her—"

"Okay, she's not a bitch. You're just a pussy."

God, please give me the strength to keep my hands off this man, Nate thought. *Because if you don't, I might be going back to that damn jail tonight.*

Nate counted to ten. His heart boomed, and he felt adrenaline singing through his blood, his muscles tense with the expectation of violence, but he kept his hands buried in his pockets, and he kept his feet in place.

Glowering at him, Marvin squeezed his hands into fists. His nostrils flared.

"To hell with this," Nate said. "I'm done here."

"I'm *not* done. I know what you did. You owe me."

"What the hell are you talking about?" Nate said, but dread plucked his heart.

"Your letter to the school. I know what you did. Everything that happened that day. It's on you." He pointed at Nate.

"That . . . that was a long time ago. I was a kid."

"So was I. Look at the price I'm still paying, motherfucker."

"I was only trying to help, Marvin! Your stepdad was beating the hell out of you. Someone had to say something."

"He beat the hell out of me when we got home, too. Really went in with his fists that time. Told me all about the letter and the call he got from the school. He thought *I* wrote it."

"You?" Nate's head felt as if it would implode. "God, I'm sorry, man. I was only trying to help."

"I go to prison, and you go to college." Marvin sneered. "Yeah, you *helped*, Nathan. Appreciate that, brother."

"I can't take it back now. What do you want me to do? I gave you a job, I bailed you out of jail, I've put you up in this motel. What else do you expect from me, huh?"

"I've been considering some things. We could start with your buying me a new car. Don't tell me you can't afford it because we know that's a damn lie."

"I'm going home." Nate retreated toward his truck. "I'm not doing this with you tonight."

"Run home to your bitch, pussy. You wouldn't last one night in the joint, in the real world. You're soft as cotton."

"Fuck you!"

Marvin pointed at Nate as he got in his truck.

"You owe me!" Marvin shouted, his voice audible despite the pouring rain.

He was still pointing at Nate and shouting as Nate screeched out of the motel parking lot.

24

Leslie was still awake when Nate arrived home, watching Netflix in the family room and sipping a cup of tea, a blanket wrapped around her shoulders. Striding back and forth across the area rug, too wound up to sit, Nate told her what had happened.

He felt as if he needed to smash something. He snatched a throw pillow off the sofa and squeezed it in both hands as he paced and talked.

Marvin had pushed him to the brink of violence, and the adrenaline still simmered in his blood. Nate hadn't felt that close to a physical altercation since he'd been a kid. It scared the shit out of him. He had too much to lose, and, he reminded himself, Marvin had nothing to lose.

"I don't like this at all," Leslie said when he finished. She set her mug on an end table and wrapped the blanket around her more tightly. "This foolishness about you owing him. His prior restraining orders. This is bad news, babe."

"I never should have bailed him out," Nate said. "His sister warned me about it."

Leslie only looked at him, lips pursed.

"Yeah, I know, you told me the same thing," he said. "You don't need to remind me."

"What's done is done."

"I was only trying to do the right thing, keep my word. He wouldn't have started the fight if he hadn't been at my store in the first place."

"Do you still believe you owe him something?" Leslie said.

I go to prison, and you go to college.

Nate halted in mid-step. He pressed his hand against his throbbing head.

"I don't know," he said.

"That sounds like a yes," Leslie said.

"His stepdad thought *Marvin* wrote that letter. I don't know why he would have thought that . . . I don't know. I can't remember what I wrote. It was—"

"Thirty years ago." Her calm gaze fixed on him, Leslie picked up her teacup and sipped.

"Right. A long time ago."

"You were a child. You need to let this go."

"But Marvin hasn't let it go. He made that pretty damn clear tonight, threw it all in my face."

Finally out of gas, Nate settled next to her on the sofa. He knotted his clammy hands in his lap.

He wished he had never run into Marvin again. Talk about the chance encounter from hell. Why was trying to do right by someone leading to one terrible outcome after another? Life wasn't supposed to work like that. Good deeds were supposed to be rewarded, weren't they?

Despite what had happened so far, Nate didn't see any way he could have avoided ending up here. He was the kind of guy who gladly reached out to help a friend in need; he strived always to keep his promises. He was generous with his time, his money, his energy.

Why is this happening to me? What did I do to deserve this?

Leslie edged closer to him and rubbed her hand across his back, kneading his muscles.

"You're so tense," she said.

"I'm exhausted and I have a headache, but I won't get any sleep tonight."

"You can take one of my pills, if you want."

Leslie occasionally suffered from insomnia and had a sleep medicine prescription; on more than one occasion, when work stress got to him, he took her up on the offer.

"Thanks, but not tonight," he said.

"You're worried Marvin might show up here?"

He shifted to look at her.

"It's not over between us," he said. "It feels like tonight was the first shot across the bow; the masks are finally off, and this guy doesn't have a damn thing to lose, Les."

25

On Saturdays, Nate's UPS Stores opened to the public at ten o'clock in the morning. But that day, Nate arrived at his Norcross location around eight, at least an hour earlier than usual, though he planned to open at the regular time.

As expected, he'd slept fitfully. When he slipped away at some point into slumber, he dreamed about being twelve again, riding bikes with Marvin on a sunny afternoon, laughing and carefree as they raced along bicycle trails.

The nostalgic dream felt like a cruel joke.

Last night's rain had ended, and the morning was clear and spangled with sunshine, though the temperature hovered in the forties and a blustery wind gusted. The first thing Nate noticed when he pulled into the shopping center parking lot—and the first thing he looked for, honestly, and his entire reason for getting there so early—was Marvin's Oldsmobile Cutlass Supreme. It had been parked near the store.

The car was gone.

Had it been towed? Or had Marvin returned and somehow coaxed the old car to start?

Nate parked his truck near the spot the Oldsmobile had occupied. He sipped coffee from his thermos—he was on his second cup, already—and the brew felt like hot acid.

This new development worried him.

He climbed out of the truck. Hands on his waist, he scanned the parking lot.

He spotted two vehicles that appeared to have been parked there overnight: condensation filmed the windows, and dead leaves clotted the windshield wipers. They hadn't been towed.

Marvin came back and got his car.

Marvin could have hired a towing service to retrieve his vehicle, but that seemed ludicrous. He didn't have any money; he was broke as a joke.

How do you know he's broke? Have you seen his bank statement, Nate?

It struck Nate how little he knew about Marvin, the grown-up. Since they had reconnected, most of their conversation had been surface chatter, punctuated with Marvin's occasional quasi-philo-sophical musings about "the system."

His sister, Danielle, might have some insight. But the idea of contacting her sent a pleasant shiver down his spine, a feeling he didn't entirely trust.

He turned and headed toward his store. As he unlocked the front door, he noticed the security camera posted above the doorway. It gave him an idea.

Once settled inside, he opened the store's security system moni-toring app on his phone, a separate application from the Ring app he used for his house.

The camera network surveilled the store's rear, interior, and entrance. After yesterday's blowup, he entertained himself by reviewing footage of Marvin's rampage inside the business. His old friend trashed packages and flipped over the printer like a man in a roid rage. He even had footage of Marvin racing off from the loading dock to attack his former manager, though the actual assault occurred outside the camera's range.

The camera above the front entrance provided a partial view of the parking lot; the live shot showed the back of Nate's truck.

He scrolled through the recorded footage. At 2:18 a.m., a hooded figure appeared near the Oldsmobile, opened the trunk, and retrieved several items.

Seventeen minutes later, the same figure returned things to the trunk and drove away in the car.

Son of a bitch, Nate thought.

26

———

When the doorbell chimed, Pamela Noble was preparing to step outside her townhouse and begin her morning walk.

Weather and health permitting, Pamela prioritized enjoying a brisk stroll outdoors almost daily. At sixty-five years old, she was in better shape than ever. In her youth, the responsibilities of raising two children, maintaining their home, and working full-time had left precious little time for extracurricular activities like taking a daily walk.

She was sitting on the sofa, lacing up her running shoes, when the doorbell rang. She glanced at her Apple Watch; it was nine o'clock, and she wasn't expecting any visitors.

A couple of years ago, her son had installed a Ring system at her home. She picked up her phone and opened the app to access the front door camera.

It was Marvin Waters.

What an interesting coincidence, Pamela thought. Last night, she'd dreamt of the young man. She couldn't remember the precise content of the dream, but whatever it was, it disturbed her. But was that surprising considering the terrible thing that had happened when he was a child?

She might not have recognized Marvin if her son hadn't texted her a photo last week. In the pic, the two of them shook hands while standing inside Nate's store, Marvin proudly wearing a UPS Store uniform. It had filled Pamela with pride that her son had the means and the character to offer employment to his old friend.

Pamela rose from the sofa and hurried to the door. As a rule, she never opened the door for strangers, but this young man was no stranger. She had known his mother well and she had fond memories of Marvin, too.

Marvin wore a tattered black fleece jacket, wrinkled jeans, and scuffed sneakers. As an adult, he didn't have his mother's looks—his sister had inherited those—but his smile was as bright as the morning sunshine.

"Good morning, Ms. Noble," he said. "Do you know who I am?"

"Of course I know who you are, baby!" she said. "Mister Marvin Waters, all grown up. Look at you! Get in here and gimme a hug!"

His grin broadening, Marvin stepped inside her home.

27

"Nathan gave me your address, ma'am," Marvin said as she ushered him down the hallway and into the kitchen. "I happened to be passing through the area and thought I'd drop by to say hello, and thankfully, you're home. It's so wonderful to see you again, Miss Noble."

"You as well, sweetheart, you as well." Pamela gestured to the dinette table. "Please have a seat. Can I get you a cup of coffee, dear? Tea?"

"Coffee would be lovely, but I won't be staying long. I know you weren't expecting my visit."

As he settled into a chair, Pamela retrieved a ceramic mug from the cabinet and dropped a pod into her Keurig coffee maker. She glanced over her shoulder and saw Marvin scanning the kitchen with an attentive gaze that seemed to take in everything. It reminded her of when he would come inside their home as a child; he was a studious, quiet boy who never missed a detail, and it was such a shame that his life had been derailed.

"You have a lovely home, ma'am," Marvin said.

"Thank you." Coffee gurgled into the cup. "Cream and sugar?"

"Both, please. Thank you so much."

Pamela brought the coffee, cream, and sugar to the table, and Marvin thanked her again in his soft voice. He'd been a well-mannered child, and she was grateful that life had not robbed him of his grace.

Marvin sipped the beverage. "This is perfect."

"I was so upset when I learned of your mother's passing," Pamela said. "In our school days, we were very close, almost like you and my son."

"I believe I recall her saying something to that effect." A cloud passed over Marvin's gaze. "I miss her every day."

"I understand. I was close to my mama, too."

Holding the mug in both hands, Marvin leaned forward. "If I may ask, do you have my mother's obituary?"

"I do. I took it out last weekend to show it to Nate. Give me a moment."

"Thank you, ma'am."

Pamela padded out of the kitchen and went upstairs. In her study, she found the scrapbook where she kept various documents she had collected over the years, including a growing number of obituaries of family and friends. She fished out the well-preserved pamphlet.

When she returned to the kitchen, she found Marvin standing near the refrigerator, looking at family photos she had fastened to the door with miscellaneous magnets. Her intuition suggested that he had snooped around while she had been away, but was that so unusual? Of course he was curious. He hadn't been inside any house of hers in thirty years.

"Nice photographs here," he said. "Grandkids?"

"Yes, my daughter's children. Nate hasn't blessed me with any kids yet, but with this marriage to Leslie coming up, I'm hopeful."

"He's a lucky man. I've never walked down the aisle myself." He shrugged. "A rolling stone gathers no moss, like Mama used to say."

She offered him the obituary. He accepted it with a slight, gracious bow.

"You can keep it," she said. "I have a couple of other copies."

"Thank you." Marvin carefully placed the pamphlet on the counter and traced his index finger across the photo of his mother on the front page. She could see emotions at war on his scarred face.

She wanted to figure out a way to respectfully ask why he had missed the funeral, but before she could broach the topic, he spoke again.

"I'm still upset that I missed Mama's service," he said.

"Come to think of it, I don't remember seeing you there."

"Yes." Marvin lowered his head as if shame continued to plague him. "I'd been struck with a sudden case of pneumonia the day before the funeral. Spent three nights at Grady Hospital."

"Oh, dear," Pamela said. "I'm so sorry."

"My sister and I had a falling-out over my absence." Marvin drew in a breath and wiped his misty eyes. "We still haven't repaired our relationship; there's been a tension between us ever since. Mama was the glue that held us together."

"Death takes a terrible toll on the family. But you have time to mend things with your sister."

"You're so wise, Miss Noble. It's no wonder Nathan found such great success in life having you in his corner." Marvin sipped coffee, then placed the cup on the counter. "It's been great reconnecting with him, despite what happened recently."

"What happened?" she asked.

"He hasn't shared this with you?"

Pamela shook her head.

"He's intending to terminate my employment over a misunderstanding. He promised me he'd help me get back on my feet, and I depended on his assistance." Marvin dabbed at his mouth with a napkin. "I should have learned by now that I'm alone in this cold world and can't rely on anyone. I'll manage like I always have, but I had such high hopes considering how long we've known each other. He was my best friend, you know."

"I didn't know anything about that, Marvin. I'll talk to him."

"Would you? I'd appreciate that so much, ma'am. I feel like we're almost like family, yes?"

"My son will try his best to do right by you."

"I ought to get going, ma'am. Thank you for your hospitality."

"Anytime."

He tucked the obituary into his jacket pocket. Pamela walked him to the front door and drew him into another embrace.

"It was so good to see you again, Marvin. I'll be sure to let Nate know you stopped by."

"You do that." Marvin beamed. "I'm sure he'll be surprised."

28

———————

"Sorry, boss, your friend lied to you," Denise said to Nate. Her olive-skinned complexion reddened. "How dare that jerk accuse *me* of theft?"

Denise had arrived at the Norcross location before they opened their doors to the public. She seemed surprised to find Nate already there—she was scheduled to open that day—but Nate explained that he was investigating some matters with Marvin. He didn't bother bringing up the business with Marvin's car. But he wanted to see her response when he told her about Marvin's accusation that he'd seen her stealing printer cartridges.

Her reaction told Nate what he needed to know.

"I had to ask you," Nate said. "I didn't believe it."

"Let's check inventory, boss." Denise spun from the front counter and marched down the hallway to the large storage closet. "If anything's not adding up, he's probably why."

In the storage room, they counted the number of printer cartridges in stock, and then Denise pulled up the latest count using their inventory management software.

"We're short four units, not two." Nate studied the computer screen in the administrative office. He grimaced. "That guy."

"I didn't take them," Denise said. Sitting in the office chair before the laptop, she swiveled to face Nate. "I hope you believe me."

Her face was still flushed red; he could see how much the accusation stung her. He could have strangled Marvin. Finding good employees without interrogating them about false charges was hard enough.

"I'm sorry I had to even bring this up with you," he said. "I never believed it, but I needed to follow through."

"Can I speak freely?" she asked.

"Of course you can."

Her eyes tightened. "I hope you'll *fire* your friend. After what he did yesterday and now this, he's bad news, boss. Truly."

"You won't be seeing him in here again, Denise. That's a promise."

"What a relief." She blew out a loud breath and flicked hair out of her face. "But are you two still friends? You said you've known each other since you were kids."

We go back like rocking chairs, Nathan . . .

He winced as if the idea was painful. "That's a tough question. We're not in a good place."

"I mean, you tried. You gave him a job. He creeped me out from the start."

"What do you mean? What did he do?"

She brushed a strand of hair out of her face again, a nervous gesture. "He was a flirt. Not with me, mind you—I guess I wasn't his type. But when we had lady customers come in that he thought were attractive, he'd be gushing over them. It was totally inappropriate."

"Flirting with customers, wow. That's so out of bounds."

"I warned him about it in a nice way, and he blew me off. He said you and him were tight, and he could do whatever he wanted."

"Whatever he wanted," Nate said. He almost laughed.

"Oh, yeah, he'd make these snarky little comments about it, too.

He said he would be managing all the stores one day because you guys went way back. Once, he said you owed him so much, you would make him a co-partner."

Nate's mind spun. "Co-partner?"

"I wasn't going to mention it. I figured it was something between you guys."

"He was lying. He's done here, and I never promised him anything about being a co-partner."

"What do you owe him, though, boss? If you don't mind my asking? Marvin was adamant about that. He said it a few times."

As Nate weighed how to answer, his phone buzzed. He slipped it out of his pocket and found a text from his mother.

"Guess who visited me this morning? Marvin!"

29

———

"Tell me everything about this visit, Mom," Nate said. He'd excused himself from the store and returned to his truck to call his mother, broadcasting their conversation over Bluetooth. He clenched and unclenched his hands in his lap as they spoke.

"Is everything okay, Nate?" Mom asked. He could tell from her labored breathing and the sporadic wind gusts that she was walking outdoors.

"We'll get to that. Please, tell me everything."

"I was about to go out for my morning walk, and he rang the doorbell. I wouldn't have recognized him if you hadn't sent me that photo last week. I let him in. He's not a stranger."

Actually, he is *a stranger*, Nate thought, but he let his mother continue.

"He was very polite," Mom said. "I offered him a cup of coffee and he took it. He asked for his mother's obituary, and I gave him one of my copies. He said he had pneumonia and missed the funeral."

"Pneumonia, huh?" Nate asked.

"Is that the truth?"

"I don't know. What else?"

"He said he and his sister had a falling-out over him missing their mother's service. I told him he should work on that relationship. Family's so important, you know?"

"What else, Mom?"

"He said you fired him. Is that true? He's very upset about it."

Coming from his mother, the words were like a gut punch.

"It's between you two," Mom continued before he could respond. "I've never meddled in your business before, but it's clear that Marvin's lived a difficult life. He was counting on you."

"This is such bullshit," Nate said, more to himself than to his mother.

"Excuse me?" Mom asked, her tone sharp.

He felt twelve years old again, risking a reprimand for using an obscene word in his mom's presence.

"Sorry," he said. "What else did Marvin say?"

"He thanked me for my hospitality, and then he left. What's going on between you boys?"

Nate told his mother everything, leaving out only the details of his argument at the motel with Marvin last night: *"You owe me!"* Mom knew nothing about that old letter, and he didn't want to bring it up with her. What difference would it make now?

Still, he regretted not sharing the latest details with her before this morning. He had never expected Marvin to track down his mom's address and arrive at her house.

You've gotta get with it, Nate. The asshole dropped in for an unannounced visit at your own house, too, remember?

And in the next heartbeat, Nate thought: *He's up to something, but I don't know what.*

"He seemed so polite, like the child I remember," Mom said when he finished his story.

"People change, Mom. He's not that sweet little boy anymore. He's trouble."

"It hurts my heart to think of him like that," she said. "I know Rachel wanted the best for him." She hesitated. "Did I ever tell you that she and I were pregnant with you boys at the same time?"

"I think I'm a month older than he is," he said. "But I don't remember you saying anything about it."

"It was a long time ago. His mother and I were close before she hooked up with that jerk. He shut her off from all her friends. He was a control freak."

"Who was Marvin's biological father?" Nate asked. "He's never told me. I don't think he knows him. Sort of like my situation."

"A deadbeat," Mom said, a note of finality in her tone. "Yes, exactly like your father, Nate."

The topic of his dad remained a sore spot with his mother after all these years. Nate had mostly moved past it—he didn't know if his father was even alive. He'd never met the man or anyone on the paternal side of his family. He had turned out fine despite his father's absence, thanks to his mother's steady hand and a solid male role model in his uncle Rob, who'd owned a string of barbershops and preached the virtues of business ownership to Nate. Sometimes, Nate believed his absent father had helped him become more resilient.

But that wasn't the outcome for everyone: Marvin being the perfect case in point. How might his friend's life have turned out if his biological father had been a strong, positive influence? Or if Leon Waters, his stepdad, had been a decent guy and not a violent abuser?

"If Marvin contacts you again, shows up at your house, or anything else, please let me know," Nate said.

"Our families have a history. I want you to remember that and do the right thing here, Nathaniel."

His mother used his full name only when she was deadly serious.

"I will," he said. "Promise."

30

Immediately after Nate wrapped up his troubling call with his mother, he called Marvin.

I'm going to set this asshole straight once and for all, he thought. *Visiting my mom is crossing the line.*

He had no idea how Marvin had located his mother, but it didn't surprise him. The guy was fiendishly clever and resourceful, and you could find almost anything online if you knew where to look.

But *why* had Marvin visited Mom? What was his angle? Marvin's request for his deceased mother's obituary felt like a ruse. What was he after?

Mucking up things with my family. Putting pressure on me. That's what he wants.

The phone rang and rang, and soon clicked into voicemail. Nate terminated the call.

Tremors shook his hands. His clammy fingers left smudges on the phone's screen as he texted Marvin.

The message: *"Stay away from my mother. You've been warned."*

That was all he needed to say, Nate decided. Writing more would dilute the impact.

After he sent the text, he stared at the display, his jaws bulging with tension. But Marvin didn't reply, and he didn't call back, either.

Nate pictured Marvin, phone glued to his hand, as he purposely ignored Nate's call, and now reading the text. Was Marvin scared now? Or was his silence the equivalent of a big, fat middle finger to Nate?

Nate veered out of the shopping center parking lot and drove at a high speed to the motel down the road where he had booked a three-night stay for Marvin. Marvin's car wasn't there, and Nate realized how foolish it had been for him to come there to look; Marvin was clear on the other side of metro Atlanta near his mom's place, at least a thirty-minute drive away.

"Cool it, Nate," he whispered to himself. "Don't let him trigger you."

Instead of returning to the Norcross store, Nate swung by a Chik-fil-A drive-through and ordered breakfast: two chicken biscuits and hash browns. He usually skipped breakfast and got by on strong coffee and ice water until lunch, but nervous energy had stoked his appetite. He tore through the food while sitting in his truck, ignoring his own rule about eating inside his vehicle, and then he doubled back to the Norcross store.

"Everything okay, boss?" Denise asked when he came in.

She had opened the shop by then and had a customer at the counter with a package, but her brow furrowed as she regarded him.

"All good." Nate gave her and the curious customer a forced smile. "I'll be in the back."

In the administrative office, he shut the door.

He had a million work tasks ahead of him, and he needed to visit his other stores. Saturday might have been a day off for the typical nine-to-five worker, but for Nate, it was one of the busiest days of the week.

Before focusing on business, he needed to handle his personal life.

He opened the file cabinet drawer containing personnel files, thumbed through the labeled tabs, and pulled out Marvin's employment records.

In hindsight, he felt like an idiot for ignoring Leslie's advice to run a background check on his friend. Hadn't Marvin's sister hinted that he had done things that would blow Nate's mind?

I need to know who I'm up against.

Under normal circumstances, receiving a comprehensive background check report from the screening vendor he used could take several days, sometimes weeks. Calling Danielle to learn about these cryptic "mind-blowing" details would have been faster, but he was reluctant to contact her.

He would follow his standard protocol for such things, and this time, he would pay the screening firm to expedite the results.

31

_____

On Saturday afternoon, Leslie visited Sugarloaf Mills, an indoor shopping mall in Lawrenceville, to browse for wedding-related clothing. She'd purchased her bridal dress already—a stunning outfit that would knock Nate off his feet—but other pieces demanded her attention: clothes for the wedding shower, bachelorette party, and rehearsal dinner, for starters. Her motto for the wedding: Go big, or go home.

Time raced by, the Big Day approaching with relentless speed. As far as Leslie was concerned, it couldn't get here fast enough.

She had created a name for her newfound anxiety: the Marvin Situation.

Nate's deranged childhood friend loomed like an X factor that had invaded their lives, threatening to spoil their plans.

Marvin's disturbances had piled up over the past week or so: his lecherous behavior upon meeting Leslie, showing up uninvited at their house to leave a bizarre gift, wreaking havoc at Nate's business, choking a man and punching Nate in the face (no accident, Leslie was sure), landing in jail, then threatening Nate over a thirty-year-old grudge after Nate bailed him out.

The Marvin Situation cast a bleak shadow over their future. It buzzed in Leslie's mind like a broken fan clattering in a musty cellar. She couldn't repair or silence it, which grated against her instinct to tackle problems head-on. This time, she had to trust Nate to handle it. She could offer advice, but ultimately, the Marvin Situation fell to Nate to solve.

Unfortunately, Nate's natural kindness and trust left him vulnerable to exploitation. Marvin had already taken advantage.

And now, Marvin had escalated the situation, as Nate himself admitted.

Maybe this explained why Leslie felt eyes on her as she traveled through the mall. That unmistakable sensation of being watched tickled the back of her neck. But each time she looked around, no one stood out. Had anxiety morphed into paranoia?

After an hour of window-shopping and buying a few discounted pieces—retail therapy in action—Leslie headed to the food court. She picked up teriyaki chicken, white rice, and vegetables from a hibachi spot and settled at a small table flanked by plastic chairs. She pushed the rice aside with her disposable fork and picked at the other food. Refined carbs were the enemy; she had to fit into that size six dress in one hundred and twelve days.

"Hello there, Miss Lady," a voice said behind her.

Leslie froze, fork suspended above her plate.

Marvin slithered into the chair across from her, the mingled odors of cigarette smoke and cheap cologne trailing him like a tail. Here was the Marvin Situation, up close and personal.

Leslie gripped the utensil like a weapon with her right hand. Her left reached for her phone.

"You've been stalking me," she said—a statement, not a question.

"Admiring you from afar. What can I say? Nathan's a lucky brother, Miss Lady."

"I know everything you've done. You're lucky he didn't leave your crazy ass in jail."

Marvin flinched as if slapped. Leslie savored the small victory but thought: *Careful, girl.* She knew from Nate's experience with Marvin that this guy had an explosive temper, and he could erupt at any moment, public setting be damned.

She scanned her surroundings. About twenty yards away, a security guard stood posted near the restrooms. The man looked ancient, but the radio on his hip offered a lifeline if things went wrong.

"You're trying to provoke me," Marvin said, scratching his bearded chin. "But I'm not going back to jail. You might play Nathan like a fiddle, but those simple-ass tricks won't work on me, girlfriend. I'm smarter than you."

"Why the hell are you following me? What do you want?"

"I come on a mission of mercy." Marvin spread his arms wide. "I'm your guardian angel, Miss Lady, your knight in shining armor."

Leslie scowled. Was he high on something more potent than nicotine?

"You've got one minute," she said. "Talk like you've got some sense."

"Nathan and I had a heart-to-heart about your upcoming nuptials." Marvin's hands rested on the table, but he fidgeted and snatched one of her napkins to twist and braid between his long fingers. Nicotine withdrawal radiated from him.

"So what?" she said. "You think you're getting an invitation? Not happening, Marvin."

"Nathan's got cold feet."

Leslie's pulse quickened. "Excuse me?"

"Nathan and I go back like rocking chairs." Marvin leaned back as if expecting his plastic seat to rock. "It doesn't matter that we didn't see each other for thirty years. We have a connection. We're family. My boy said he's got serious doubts about meeting you at the altar."

"You're lying. He didn't tell you that."

Though she spat the words with deserved venom, nausea churned in her gut. She clenched her jaws.

He's lying! You know that, girl. He's manipulating you.

But his words struck her deepest fear about the wedding. She'd been abandoned at the altar before. Nate loved her—she knew that with certainty. But his disinterest in wedding planning and constant excuses for skipping appointments had triggered a simmering anxiety that she'd be standing alone on the Big Day.

"I'm done with this nonsense," Leslie said.

"Don't shoot the messenger, Miss Lady," Marvin said with a shrug, feigning indifference.

Leslie's hands shook as she gathered her things and stood. Her knees wobbled, forcing her to steady herself against the table.

"Stop following me." She jabbed a finger at him. "Or I'll call the police and slap another restraining order on you. Yeah, I know about that, too, jailbird."

Marvin lit a cigarette, ignoring the indoor smoking ban.

"I said what I meant to say," he said. "Do what you will with this information. My advice? Keep a close watch on my friend. He's got a wandering eye, too."

"If I see you again, you'll be in big trouble," she said. "Watch yourself, asshole."

Marvin blew smoke toward her as she marched away.

32

Nate's original plan for dinner that evening was to grill some dry-aged rib eye steaks, crack open a good cabernet and bourbon, and sit down with Marvin and Leslie in their house's spacious, well-heated sunroom. He'd picked up the food a couple of days ago before everything went sideways with Marvin. He resolved to cook anyway, for himself and his fiancée. Why should he allow his ongoing drama with Marvin—who still hadn't responded to his text—to spoil everything?

But Leslie seemed upset.

She avoided meeting his gaze as he worked in the kitchen. She let out frequent, loud sighs and gave him curt responses when he asked her questions.

If she kept acting like this, it would be a long night.

Nate assumed she was upset about this situation with Marvin. He had told her about Marvin visiting his mother, and Leslie had murmured only "Hmph" and shrugged as if to say, *Well, what did you expect, genius? Of course your demented friend visited your mom.*

She blamed him for it, Nate knew; she blamed him for every-thing. He couldn't argue the point with her—he'd made plenty of bad decisions, which he'd admitted. How long was she going to punish him for it?

This woman carries a grudge like nobody's business.

That was one of the things about Leslie that sometimes gave him pause when he thought about the pending marriage. He would assume a contentious issue was settled between them, but afterward, she'd start dwelling on it, and she would get upset all over again and be moody for days. Could he deal with her acting like this for the next forty years?

No one's perfect, least of all you, man.

His prior girlfriends had accused him of being a "chronic workaholic and emotionally absent" (he wasn't sure he agreed with that second part). Leslie was the first woman he had met who loved him despite his flaws. He ought to be able to look past whatever deficiencies he saw in her. It could be annoying, but it wasn't a deal-breaker.

What if something else was bothering her?

They sat down at the table across from each other. For several minutes, the only sounds were the clink of their silverware against their plates and the muted notes of an Earth, Wind & Fire track throbbing from the kitchen's Bluetooth speaker.

Leslie swiped and tapped her phone between taking small bites of her steak and grilled root vegetables. One of their agreed-upon dinner rules was no mobile devices at the table. The rule had been Leslie's idea, intended to keep him from working when they were supposed to be breaking bread together.

He couldn't take it anymore. He put down his knife and fork.

"All right," he said. "What's the deal, Les? You've been throwing serious shade at me all evening."

Leslie put down her phone. She glowered at him.

"I saw your friend today," she said.

"Marvin?"

"No, Santa Claus." Her jaws clenched as her gaze filleted him. "Yes, Marvin."

"Where?"

"He stalked me at the mall and then sat next to me when I was eating lunch. Said he was there on a mission of mercy."

"A mission of mercy? What the hell does that mean?"

"You don't know, hmm?" Leslie tilted forward against the table. "He told me all about a little chat you and him had about our wedding."

Nate ransacked his memory, trying to recall what he had said to Marvin about the marriage that could set her off.

"You still don't know?" she asked.

"Did he lie and say I invited him or something?"

"He said you have cold feet, Nate. He said you're having serious doubts about marrying me at all."

"I didn't say that!" Nate pushed away from the table so quickly that the chair behind him toppled over and crashed against the floor. "Dammit, Les, he's lying! I never told him I don't want to marry you!"

"What did you tell him, Nate?" She crossed her arms over her chest. Her gaze was cool, but her tone was colder. "Why don't you give me the fine details of your little chitchat?"

"I may have said I'll be glad when the wedding is over. I've said the same thing to you. That's all I said. If he claims I said anything else, he's lying."

She studied him cooly.

"Do you want to go through with this wedding?" she asked. "Truly. I want you to be one hundred percent honest with me."

"You've let this guy get into your head! You can't believe anything he says. He's playing you. He's playing *us*."

"And you couldn't answer my question." Leslie plucked her wineglass off the table and sipped the cabernet, draining the goblet.

"Why is this even a question now? Because some guy I really don't even know anymore made up some lies and fed these crazy doubts you've been obsessing over? I know you're worried I'm gonna stand you up at the altar, Les, but I would never, ever do that." His chest heaved. "I want to marry you!"

Tears streamed down Leslie's cheeks.

"I should believe you," she said in a broken voice. "I know I should."

He wanted to go to her then. He wanted to pull her into his arms, kiss her, assure her that everything would be okay, promise her that they would get through this together and keep moving toward the storybook wedding she had been planning for the past year.

But murmuring hollow promises wasn't going to solve their problem. Taking decisive action was going to solve the problem.

"I'll be back," he said, charging to the doorway.

She rose, too. "Where are you going now?"

"I'm going to put an end to this bullshit. Tonight."

Nate left the house before she could stop him.

33

Nate swerved into the motel's parking lot.

Far from the drive taking the edge off his anger, every mile he traveled along the night-dimmed roads pushed his fury to a higher pitch. First, Marvin had visited his mother to stir up things; now, he had targeted Leslie, stalking her and spreading lies with one diabolical purpose: to ruin Nate's life.

All for what? To compel Nate to buy him a new car and give him back his job?

As Nate drove, he clenched the steering wheel so tightly it was a miracle it didn't snap like a pretzel. He imagined the wheel was Marvin's neck.

He dimly recognized he was out of control, but he didn't want to stop it. Nothing short of putting rough hands on Marvin was going to satisfy him. Clearly, Marvin wasn't the kind of guy who'd listen to reasonable arguments and gentle persuasion. He lived in the gutter, and if he wanted to drag Nate down there into the grime with him, fine. They could do this.

Nate peeled around to the far corner of the parking lot. From there, he saw the front of the motel. A sparse collection of vehicles occupied the spaces alongside the L-shaped building.

Marvin's car was there, too, parked near the motel's exterior staircase and basking in the pale glow of a streetlamp.

Nate slammed his truck into Park and killed the ignition. His heart galloped so hard and fast he felt dizzy, and his mouth was dry.

As he reached for the door handle, his phone chimed. Someone had texted him.

He expected it to be Leslie messaging him to ask what he was doing, where he was, how to get back home, calm down, stay out of trouble—whatever. He'd talk to her when he was done.

But a glance at the display showed a different sender: Danielle.

"Hey, checking in with you. Thanks again for bailing out my brother, even though he works my last nerve. How're you doing?"

Nate exhaled. A memory of the woman's striking face pierced his hazy thoughts like a sunray. He typed a rapid response: *"I'm about to strangle him."*

A heartbeat later, the phone rang. He hesitated briefly before answering, broadcasting the call via the truck's Bluetooth.

Danielle's sultry voice enveloped him like a velvet shroud: "He's not worth it, Nate. Whatever you're thinking about doing, stop and take a breath."

His fingers tingled on the cool door handle.

"Trust me on this, sweetie," she said.

Nate turned away from the door, blew out a big gust of air, and lay his head back against the headrest.

34

———

"I've been there, done that, with my brother," Danielle continued. Like a hypnotist's, her voice was so soothing that Nate closed his eyes and exhaled another deep breath. "He knows how to push your buttons. That's what he does. He's too smart for his own good. He had me at my wit's end several times until I decided to stop the madness. I cut him off. You've got so much to lose by letting him drag you down to his level, but he doesn't have anything on the line, not a pot to piss in or a window to throw it out of, like my mama used to say. Remember that."

As Danielle spoke, the fog that had settled over Nate, powering him toward an adrenaline-fueled violent episode, faded away.

"You've got a business to operate, people who depend on you," Danielle said. "You have a woman at home who loves you. Marvin has nothing and no one, and I'm sorry, but he probably never will. He chooses that life but resents you for what you have. I don't know what he said or did to trigger you. Let it roll off your back. Brush it off your shoulder. They're only sticks and stones, like they say. Forget that, and you'll wind up next to him in a jail cell."

"Thank you." Nate cleared his throat and glanced toward the

motel. "If you hadn't reached out to me when you did, God help me."

"I have a sixth sense for things sometimes . . . when I have a special connection with someone."

The statement hung between them. Nate cleared his throat again, but Danielle spoke first.

"Where are you?" she asked. "It sounds like you're in a car."

He laughed sourly. "I'm sitting in the parking lot of the motel I paid for your brother to stay in. I was going to bust in there and . . ." His voice trailed off.

"I know." Her voice was like a soft mitten.

"Do you want to know what happened?"

"Not if it's going to upset you all over again," she said. "Does it matter?"

He considered. "You're right. It doesn't matter."

"Go home, Nate."

"Thanks for reaching out, Danielle."

"For the last time, call me Danny, sweetie," she said, punctuating her reminder with a giggle. "I'll check in on you tomorrow. And hey, you call me anytime you need a listening ear, you hear?"

He wasn't sure how Leslie would feel about that, but he said, "I appreciate it. Goodnight, Danny."

After ending the call, Nate lifted his gaze to the window of the room Marvin had lodged in. The curtains were peeled back; he was confident he saw Marvin standing at the glass, his cigarette glowing like an ember in the darkness.

He's not worth it, Nate.

Nate started his truck and drove home.

35

That night, Nate had an electrifying erotic dream. He hadn't experienced such a powerfully vivid, sexual reverie in years, and when he woke, he ran his fingers down to check the front of his pajama shorts. He worried he had let loose at the peak of the fantasy and soiled his clothes.

Mercifully, his shorts were dry, but he had a lingering erection.

Call me Danny, sweetie.

Usually, if he remembered dreams, they vanished from his mind within seconds of waking. Not this one. He could still feel her touch and the sensation of her body against his and could hear her throaty whisper in his ear as clearly as if she were lying next to him.

But Leslie was sleeping next to him. She was his one and only, the love of his life, the woman he was due to wed in only a few months.

But the last figments of the dream echoed like crashing waves in his body.

The bedside clock read 5:04 a.m. He was too keyed up to get back to sleep, so he hit the shower, turning the temp to a colder range. The cool water dampened his libido.

When he shuffled out of the master bath, Leslie was still asleep.

She'd barely spoken to him when he'd returned home last night after his impulsive drive to the motel, and he wasn't sure today would be any better. They would have to find a way to put this Marvin Situation behind them.

When chaos took over his personal life, Nate resorted to what he always did: he went to work. He brewed a cup of strong coffee and settled into his home office in front of his laptop.

The screening vendor hadn't yet processed his background check order on Marvin, but that was to be expected. Even when expedited, the report could take time to arrive.

Another alternative surfaced in his mind, but he shut it off. No, he would wait this out. Do things the right way.

Sipping coffee, Nate worked through his unread emails and pending administrative tasks, and soon, he lost track of time. It wasn't until he heard Leslie padding downstairs that he looked up and realized that over three hours had passed.

He met her in the kitchen as she dropped a pod into the coffee brewer. She wore a green kimono robe and slippers, her hair wrapped in a pink silk bonnet.

"Good morning," he said. "Sleep well?"

The glare she gave him when she turned toward him answered his question. He felt a rock roll over his heart.

She's still mad at you, like you knew she'd be. Holding that grudge, man.

"I need caffeine." She yawned.

"Hey, I was thinking. I want to go to church with you and your mom today."

The idea had come to him as a tactic to get back into Leslie's good graces. It had been at least six months since he'd last joined her for Sunday service at her family's Baptist church in southwest Atlanta. His habitual skipping of church services was one of those things she claimed she had eventually accepted about him, but he knew she wished he attended more often.

But this suggestion brought another scowl.

"You hate going to my church," she said. "You'll sit there the entire time checking your phone and asking me when it's going to be over so you can go back to work."

Nate winced. Did he actually behave like that?

"I'm willing to set aside work and go, Les," he said. "I won't bug you about when it's going to be over, either, no matter how endless it feels." He forced a slight chuckle.

"Some other time." She glanced away from him and busied herself stirring sugar-free cream into her coffee. "I've got some things I need to talk to Mom about."

He didn't like the sound of that.

"What things?" he asked.

She shook her head. "I'm not getting into this with you right now. It's too early."

"Whatever. I'll go to work, then."

"You do that."

Without another glance at him, Leslie padded out of the kitchen, leaving him alone to ponder how he would fix this.

36

Danielle texted him around eleven. Nate was at his UPS Store in Lawrenceville, assisting the store manager with an inventory review.

When he saw Danielle's name pop up on the screen, he felt a charge of excitement. Last night's dream, still fresh, flickered like an HD movie clip through his mind.

"Hi, just checking in with you. I know yesterday was rough. How're you doing?"

Nate excused himself and went outside through the loading bay door in the back of the building. Holding the phone in front of him, he stared at the screen.

She sent another message: *"Can you talk now?"*

He drew in a deep breath—and called her. She answered immediately.

"Hey, you," she said.

Hearing her low, warm voice was like being wrapped in a velvety blanket. His heart throbbed a little faster.

"Hey," he said. "When we met the other day, you mentioned that

Marvin had done things that would blow my mind. What things, exactly?"

"Hmm." She clucked her tongue. "That's a heavy subject to talk about on the phone."

"Sorry, I understand it's a complicated question, but I need to know."

"Can you meet me somewhere? For lunch?"

"Lunch?" He felt another quickening of his pulse. "Today?"

"Is today good for you? I know you're a busy guy. I can find a sitter—my neighbor's home, and my son adores her."

They agreed to meet at one o'clock at an Applebee's in Lawrenceville.

Nate didn't depart the store until one because he got entangled in a challenging print order from a customer, but he texted Danielle to let her know he was delayed.

She responded: *"No worries, already seated and chillin'. Can't wait to see you again."*

Her comment—*can't wait to see you again*—boomeranged through his thoughts as he drove to the restaurant. This wasn't a date. Was she clear on that? He was meeting her for the sole purpose of mining additional information about her brother. It wasn't a prelude to romance.

So why was his heart rate elevated according to his Apple Watch?

He spotted Danielle right away when he stepped inside the restaurant. She was seated at a booth near a bank of windows. As he approached, she slid out of her seat to greet him.

She wore a knitted white scoop-neck sweater and black denim jeans. He couldn't help noticing how tightly those clothes fit her—and how they flattered every exquisite inch of her body.

When they hugged, and he felt her soft cheek press briefly against his, his dream flooded back into his mind.

"You smell amazing," she said after their embrace as she lowered back into her seat. "What cologne is that?"

"Something my fiancée bought me last Christmas. I don't remember what it's called."

"I see." Her eyes danced with what he interpreted as amusement. "Your fiancée has good taste."

A server visited their table. Nate ordered a Coke and requested time to review the menu.

Watching him, Danielle sipped her ginger ale through a straw, her lips puckered. Her burgundy lipstick left a faint smear on the plastic when she slipped the straw out of her mouth.

He cleared his throat.

"Do you have the day off?" he asked. "You mentioned you hold down two jobs."

"Today, I'm off. But so you know, in job number one, I'm a medical assistant at an urgent care clinic in Norcross. My other job is in retail at a boutique—I get discounts on cute clothes and flexible hours." With her delicate fingers, she stirred the straw in the tall glass. "It's a living. I've gotta do whatever's necessary to care for my little man."

"I get that. Is his father involved? Sorry if that's too personal."

"He's not involved." She shrugged her narrow shoulders. "It's only me. No baby daddy in the picture, no man living with me. It's me and my son against the world."

"A single mother raised me. I think I turned out all right."

"Better than all right, I'd say." She laughed. "I've met your mother, Nate. She came to Mama's service. She's a sweetheart. You were so fortunate. Not everyone has that."

He paused. "You didn't have a good relationship with your mother?"

"I don't like to speak ill of the deceased," Danielle said in a hushed tone. "But my brother has many of her ways. Mama was damaged, I guess. For different reasons."

"I knew she and my mom used to be close, but I didn't know anything else about her. I'm sorry."

"No need to apologize, sweetie." Danielle made a dismissive gesture. "You wanted to know about my brother. Let's order lunch, and I'll give you the scoop."

37

"Dang it," Danielle said. She looked at her phone, her face wrinkled with irritation. "The guy who was supposed to come put together our bookcase said he needs to reschedule. This is the second time he's canceled on me."

They had been talking for over an hour. Nate's mind spun from the colorful yet disturbing stories she shared with him about Marvin. The sum of them: as he suspected and had been learning, he didn't know Marvin anymore. Marvin was a con artist, a grifter with a flair for drama and a talent for deception; she warned that you couldn't trust anything he said, but he was also disorganized and impulsive. *He's a total mess,* she concluded. *But a dangerous mess. You've been warned.*

He couldn't wait to tell Leslie about what he'd discovered. They needed to prepare. But Danielle's comment just then dragged Nate's thoughts in a different direction.

"You hired someone to assemble a bookcase?" he asked.

"I bought it online. I hired this guy through Thumbtack, that handyman app?"

"I've heard of it."

"I don't like fussing with furniture and whatnot. Marvin used to put things together for us, but we're not on speaking terms right now, as you know."

"I could assemble it, Danny. I'm pretty handy and I've got some spare time today."

"You finally called me Danny." She grinned at him.

He smiled back.

"But are you sure you don't mind helping?" she asked. "I thought you were going back to your stores?"

"I can spare an hour or so."

"I think you're offering to help because you want to spend more time with me." She batted her long eyelashes.

Nate coughed into his hand. "Well, I . . . uh—"

"I'm fooling with you, Nate. I appreciate it, and I'm taking you up on the offer."

"Since you took the time to give me the scoop on Marvin, helping you out is the least I could do."

The server brought the check. Nate reached for it, but Danielle laid her hand over his. Her skin was soft like a ripe peach.

"I've got it," he said.

"Nah, let's split it. I don't want your fiancée finding a receipt and asking you who you had lunch with today."

"It's all good. I don't need to hide things from her. She's not jealous like that."

"She needs to be. It's tough for sistas out here in these streets."

Nate didn't know how to respond, but his face felt warm. He paid the bill.

"My place is about fifteen minutes from here." Danielle rose from the seat to put on her jacket.

"I've got your address. Marvin wrote your info on his application as a backup contact. But lead on."

He followed her out of the restaurant. She strolled with a gentle sway of her hips—the swaggering yet graceful walk of a woman confident in her beauty who knew she attracted loads of attention and basked in it.

Nate swallowed hard and tried not to stare.

Danielle drove a black Honda Civic. He trailed her in his truck. When they reached the modest duplex where she lived, he parked at the curb in front of the house.

He met her at the front door.

"Your neighbor's babysitting your boy?" he asked, gesturing to the other half of the duplex.

"She'll watch him for another hour or two. I texted her that a friend is coming over to do some work."

She beckoned him inside. The place was tastefully decorated, fastidiously clean, and smelled of a pleasant, lavender-laced fragrance. Framed photos, mostly of her son, filled the walls and tables. He was an adorable, brown-skinned boy with a megawatt smile.

Nate noted a large portrait near the living room entrance that included the entire old family unit: her mother, Leon Waters, a tiny Danielle sitting on her mother's lap, her hair in Afro puffs, and Marvin, perhaps ten years old. All of them wore cheesy grins and matching clothing.

"Hey, was Leon Waters your . . ."

"He was my biological father," Danielle said.

Marvin killed her father? No wonder they don't get along. Could you ever be on good terms with the person who murdered your dad?

"I'm sorry," he said. "I didn't know."

"It's okay, love. Let me hang up your jacket."

Before he could respond, she touched his shoulders to peel off his windbreaker. He allowed her to help, but alarm bells clanged in his mind.

Stay focused, Nate.

Danielle was gorgeous, obviously, but her appeal went beyond her physical appearance. She was sweet. Funny. Intelligent. Warm. Based on his interactions with her thus far, if he had met her three or four years ago, there was no question: he would be seriously involved with this woman.

But he was marrying Leslie.

In fact, he had a new proposal for Leslie that he would spring on her when he got home: she could have her Big Day as planned, but he wanted to go to the county courthouse and seal their matrimony this week. He needed to finalize their commitment for a host of reasons.

"Here we are." One hand clasping his elbow, Danielle steered him into the living room. A large cardboard box lay on an earth-tone area rug in front of a glass coffee table and a small leather sofa. She pointed. "I'd like to set it up over there to the right of the TV stand."

"Noted." He rubbed his hands together.

"Can I get you something to drink?"

"Water would be great, thanks."

As she strolled away, Nate knelt to open the box. He kept a Leatherman multi-tool clipped to the waist of his work pants. He extracted one of the blades and bent forward to slice open the cardboard flaps.

"Check you out." Danielle sashayed back into the living room carrying a tall glass of ice water. "I was going to ask if you needed something to open it, but you've already got it covered. I love a man who's prepared for whatever."

"My fiancée bought it for me." He waved the multi-tool at her. "Another Christmas gift."

"My girl is on top of things, hmm?" She smirked.

He turned back to the box. Danielle stopped beside him and placed the glass on a coaster lying on the coffee table.

Out of the corner of his eye, he noticed she had slipped off her boots and socks to go barefoot. Her toes were pedicured and decorated with a glossy red polish.

Even her feet are pretty. Go figure.

She touched his shoulder. "Do you need anything else?"

"I may need to step outside to grab my toolbox out of my truck."

"Of course, you keep tools in your truck. You're like a Boy Scout."

"Believe it or not, I spend a good portion of each week maintaining or fixing equipment at one of my stores. I'd have to pay a repair tech otherwise, so being handy saves me money."

"You're about your business. I admire that." She clasped her hands in front of her. "I may have to keep you on speed dial, honey. I've always got *something* that needs a little emergency maintenance."

"Do you?" He caught the double entendre and glanced up at her. She giggled and swatted his shoulder playfully.

"Your mind is all in the gutter," she said. "I don't roll like that. Don't get your hopes up."

"I'm going to put together this bookcase now," he said, smiling.

Their interaction kept on like that, a good-natured, low-key flirtation, for the next hour and a half while he assembled the bookcase. It reminded Nate of how things used to be between him and Leslie before the wedding planning became the center of her universe. For a woman like Danielle to unabashedly show interest in him flattered his ego; he knew she was also enjoying his attention. Leslie would have been furious if she knew what was going on, but it was all in innocent fun, he told himself.

"All done." He nudged the assembled bookcase a couple more inches on the laminate floor beside the television. "You're all set to shelve some books."

"Perfect." She traced her fingers along the empty shelves. "My son is a bookworm. I am, too. It's probably one of the only things my brother and I have in common."

"I mainly read finance and business books."

"All about that money, huh? Fiction is too boring?"

"To each his own," he said.

"Marvin always said I have an overactive imagination. I love reading wild thriller stories and trying to guess how they turn out. Usually, my ideas are better." She flicked a braid over her shoulder, her eyes twinkling. "I have a little devious streak in me."

"Is that so?"

"Uh-huh. Won't try to hide it."

She looked him up and down. He took in her complete profile, too, from the tips of her toes to her crown.

Nate, you need to get the hell out of here, pronto.

"I'm going back to the store," he said. "Thanks for giving me the goods on Marvin. It'll come in handy."

"You've been a lifesaver. Thank you."

"Happy to help."

Their gazes locked. Silence hung between them.

"I want to see you again," she said.

There it was now, right out in the open.

"You know I'm getting married, Danny," he said.

She reached for his left hand and held it in hers.

"I don't see a ring on this finger yet." She kissed his fingers.

Her lips were moist and soft. The sensations sent an electrifying shiver through him. He should have pulled away but felt as immobile as a statue.

"I feel like I've waited years for you," she said. "I know you feel it, too. It's all in your eyes."

"I'm getting married."

She stepped closer to him and moved his hand down to the curve of her hips.

"I heard you the first time," she said. "But you're here with me, hmm? And I know you want me as much as I want you. Am I lying?"

He didn't answer. His throat felt clogged up.

She curled her arms around his neck and pulled him close to her, pressing the soft fullness of her body against him. Her sweet fragrance enveloped him.

He felt as pliable as potter's clay in her arms. He slid his hands to her waist, and then, lower still, to her round, firm bottom.

His throbbing erection strained against his pants. She gently ground against it. With deliberate slowness, she placed feathery kisses on his chin, cheeks, and, finally, his lips, flicking him with her damp tongue.

"We would make beautiful babies," she whispered.

"I want you way too much. It's driving me crazy. But—"

"But you need to go."

"Yeah. Or I'll do something I'll always regret."

She tapped the tip of his bandaged nose with her finger.

"I'll see you again," she said as if it were a statement of fact.

"Bye, Danny."

"I'll walk you out."

She raked her fingers along his spine as he turned toward the door, teasing him with a taste of what he had missed.

Avoiding this woman would demand greater willpower than anything he had ever done in his life. But he would not break his vow to his fiancée.

Nate opened the door, Danielle at his side.

Marvin stood on the front walkway. He held up his phone, the camera lens targeting Nate and Danielle.

"Look at what we have here, folks!" Marvin cried like a gleeful child. "Nathan, wait until Miss Lady sees this!"

Marvin snapped photos.

38

———

To Nate, the entire situation felt surreal.

Standing outside the front door with Danielle clinging to his arm, the feel of her warm lips lingering on his face. Marvin about ten feet away, giggling like a mischievous kid as he took photos with his phone, his Oldsmobile parked at the curb in front of the duplex.

What is Marvin doing here? Hell, what am I even doing here?

"Marvin, dammit!" Danielle said. Although she was the younger sibling, her tone was reminiscent of a long-suffering parent admonishing a perpetually misbehaving child. "Knock it off!"

"Marvin, give me the phone," Nate said.

Nate didn't recognize the sound of his own voice: low and taut with danger. He raised his arm, his fingers grasping, knuckles crackling.

The next thing he knew, he raced toward Marvin.

Danielle shouted something behind him, but her voice was as dim to Nate as if it came from the other side of a long tube.

In Nate's rage-narrowed vision, he saw only Marvin, the onetime friend who had invaded his life like a biblical plague. He wanted to smash his face. Pummel him with his fists. Choke him. *Punish him.*

Marvin spun around to flee as Nate bore down on him, but he moved sluggishly with his bad knee. Nate seized Marvin by the hem of his jacket.

"Give me the goddamn phone!"

Nate threw a wild, arcing fist at Marvin. The punch connected flush with the side of Marvin's head.

Landing that blow was the best feeling Nate had in years.

Marvin staggered, weaving on the grass. But he had the presence of mind to flash a toothy grin.

"I'm calling the cops on you now, Nathan," Marvin said. He cupped the side of his face. "This is assault."

"Give me the phone!"

Nate lunged at Marvin, but he tripped over an uneven ridge on the walkway, teetered, and almost fell to the pavement. When he regained his bearings, Marvin had already scrambled to his car.

"Nate, please!" Danielle shouted. "He's not worth it!"

Nate ignored her and raced to the car. Marvin slammed the door in his face. Nate tried to open the door, but Marvin had snapped down the locks.

"Gimme the phone!"

Nate slammed his shoulder against the window. The car rocked from the impact, but the glass didn't break.

Safe inside the car, Marvin made a show of putting the phone against his ear. He pointed at Nate, smiling, and Nate could easily read his lips as he said: "*You're going to jail.*"

His eyes misted with fury, Nate swung around, searching the front yard for a big stone, a brick, something to smash open the window so he could haul Marvin out and bash his head in. If he was going to jail, Marvin was going to the coroner.

Danielle caught him then. She wrapped her arms around him, her body quaking from her tears.

"Baby, it's not worth it. Please don't throw it all away for him."

She wouldn't let him go, her head buried against his chest as she cried, and soon, the fight drained out of him. He trudged to the road and lowered himself onto the curb.

He was still sitting there when the police arrived.

39

Truthfully, Leslie wasn't shocked when her phone rang early that Sunday evening, and she saw the caller was from the Gwinnett County Department of Corrections. At any other time, she might have been stunned. But their lives had veered sideways, and this latest development felt like the new normal.

It was Nate. He was in jail.

With her phone against her ear, Leslie sank into the kitchen chair. She felt like she might continue sinking into a bottomless abyss.

She barely recognized Nate's voice. The connection was terrible as if he were calling from an underground bunker. But she got enough of the details.

He had been booked on an assault charge—against "you know who." He was confident he could make bail, but he could not get released until tomorrow, Monday, at the earliest. He asked her to call Denise, his most trusted store manager, to let her know he was "away but would be back tomorrow," and his attorney, who practiced employment law but had criminal defense connections, to help him wage a future court battle.

Leslie's head swam as the magnitude of what they faced washed over her.

"How did all this happen?" she asked. "Where did it happen? When?"

"Can't get into that right now." She heard hesitation in his voice and wondered if he was hiding something. "I'm getting out of here soon. You don't need to come until tomorrow. Don't tell your folks. Please."

In other words, *don't let your dad find out.* With her father a major investor in his business, allowing Dad to learn about this latest debacle would complicate matters further.

"They don't need to know," Leslie said. "Yet."

"I need you to be careful, too."

His words made her spine stiffen. "Marvin?"

"Watch out for him. Call the cops if you see him around."

Leslie's head pounded. She pressed her hand to her temple and shut her eyes.

"I'm sorry," he said. "I didn't intend for any of this to happen."

No, you didn't, she thought. *I'm sure you had good intentions, didn't you?*

Then she reprimanded herself for thinking such things. What would be the purpose of reminding him of his mistakes while he was incarcerated and alone?

"Just be careful, baby. We'll get through this." She licked her dry lips. "I love you—"

But her words met a dial tone. His allotted phone time was up.

Carefully, she placed her phone on the table. She put both hands in her hair and dug her fingers deep into her scalp.

And then, she screamed.

40

———

Although Leslie had the Ring app on her phone, which provided nonstop camera views of the front and back doorways, she kept looking out the window, watching out for that rusty Oldsmobile or an uninvited visitor.

Twilight had fallen. A motion-activated floodlight above the garage would have illuminated the front of the house as brightly as a sunray.

She double-checked that all the windows and doors were locked and confirmed that she had turned on the security system since arriving home.

Nate needn't have warned her about Marvin. Yesterday's stalking incident at the mall had been a wake-up call.

She hadn't told Nate, but last night, she ordered pepper spray online. When she returned this afternoon, the package was already waiting at the doorstep: the weapon was outfitted in a turquoise key chain that fit comfortably in her grasp.

She would keep it close at hand from this day forward.

She circuited the house, randomly looking out windows. With

the looming prospect of Nate spending maybe more than one night in jail, the sprawling house felt empty. Like that old-school slow jam Luther Vandross had covered and made his own: without that special someone to share it with, a house was not a home.

Toughen up, girlfriend.

But Leslie had lived alone, in an apartment and then a condo she bought, for years. She could handle a few nights alone; she could handle more than that if necessary.

But could she handle a permanent breakup?

Why are you even thinking about that? Will you cancel your engagement to the man you love over the Marvin Situation? Isn't that like letting that asshole win?

But they couldn't go on like this. *Nate was in jail.* Something had to give. She felt as if she were trapped in a slow-motion car wreck; with every passing day, something vital shattered.

What's next?

Leslie's nerves were so bad that she worried she might not get any sleep at all, and tomorrow was a workday, a busy Monday full of chatty meetings and pressing tasks. But she was afraid to fall asleep and risk missing an alert.

She drifted off to sleep, unintentionally, while lounging on the sofa in the family room watching a dating show on Netflix, something about desperate singles hooking up with old high school enemies or some absurd concept. These days you could find a show about damn near anything.

An alert on the Ring app woke her: a loud wind chime sound effect.

She snapped awake as if touched with an electric cattle prod. Her phone tumbled from her lap and clattered onto the rug.

As she muttered and reached to pick up the phone, the doorbell rang.

It was a few minutes past one o'clock in the morning.

She checked the app: it was Marvin. Who else? He wore his usual battered fleece jacket and smoked a cigarette. A bandage covered the side of his face—Nate's handiwork?

The thought gave her a charge of savage pleasure.

Gaily, Marvin waved at the doorbell camera through a screen of smoke. He toted a roll of paper beneath one arm.

"Hey, Miss Lady," he said. "Did I wake you from your beauty sleep, all alone in that big house?"

"I'm calling the police," she said into the microphone. "You've got ten seconds to get the hell out of here."

"You know, I could cut your internet, make that little camera you love go dark and have some fun with you."

"Ten . . . nine . . . eight . . ."

"All right, all right." He made a pacifying gesture.

"I'm getting a restraining order on you."

"Hold on, I've got something for you, Miss Lady." He indicated his parcel, which looked like a bundled poster. "I'm leaving it for you right here on the doorstep."

He placed the item against the door—and then he was suddenly upon the camera, his face pressed up against the lens so closely she could see the broken red blood vessels mapping his eyes.

Leslie uttered a thin scream.

"I've got my eye on you, Miss Lady," he said, voice tinny coming from the speaker but chilling her to the marrow.

She clutched her phone. "I'm calling the cops!"

Marvin waved and strolled out of view, trailing a tail of smoke. Leslie hurried to the front room and parted the blinds.

Marvin was gone. She saw no sign of him; she didn't see his old car, either. He could have parked around the corner, out of sight.

She trembled.

I can't go on like this, she thought.

She called the police. She didn't dare open the front door until the squad car arrived, and when she did, the roll of paper Marvin had left behind dropped across the threshold.

She picked it up; a rubber band held it in place. She slipped off the rubber band and unfurled the long sheet of paper.

It was another pencil sketch Marvin had created, a scene rendered with meticulous attention to detail.

"What the hell is this?" Leslie said.

41

Until that day, the closest Nate had ever come to any jail was when he had bailed out Marvin.

Now, he was a personal guest of the county.

Like a sleepwalker, Nate submitted to the arrest, Danielle crying and pleading in the background, and Marvin feigning such mortal injury that paramedics attended to him in an ambulance. Nate offered no resistance when the officers put handcuffs on him and drove him to the county jail; he was silent when authorities booked him, confiscated his possessions, and fingerprinted him; he offered a flat stare for his mug shot and quietly slipped on the orange prison jumpsuit and matching Crocs.

None of it felt real. He kept thinking—*truly believing*—that he would wake up soon and discover all of this had been a bad dream.

It wasn't until jail personnel allowed him to make his single phone call that the reality smashed him over the head like a brick.

Leslie didn't sound surprised, and the lack of shock in her voice stunned him to some semblance of awareness. That was how bad things had gotten for them, that he could be jailed, and she seemed to expect it was inevitable.

How did you wind up here, man? In jail? You? Mr. Law Abiding Citizen?

Why had he let Marvin trigger him to such fury that he lost all common sense? Marvin had played him like a banjo. He was better than this.

When he got his phone call, Nate fought to stifle tears as he related the situation to Leslie as briefly as he could. Two things were critical: concealing his interactions with Danielle and hiding the arrest from Leslie's dad. Although he hadn't cheated on Leslie, she wouldn't see it that way. Saying *I was only trying to help a friend assemble furniture* as his explanation for being in a strange woman's house would sound patently ridiculous.

And her dad? With an arrest for a violent crime on Nate's record, Mr. Clark might begin viewing his investment in Nate's burgeoning enterprise as risky and withhold much-needed capital.

Nate was assigned a cell—another dreamlike experience. Moving from a luxurious five-thousand-square-foot home to meager lodgings at the county jail was bound to make you question your reality.

His cellmate was a beanpole-thin, balding White guy in his thirties. He bore an uncanny resemblance to Aaron Paul, the actor who played Jesse in the crime drama *Breaking Bad*.

Nate had expected the guy to ask him the famous inmate question—*what're you in for, man?*—but his cellmate showed zero interest in Nate's plight. He was as twitchy as a malfunctioning robot and ranted nonstop about his ex-girlfriend, who he claimed had set him up on a drug possession charge so she could retain custody of their daughter.

All bitches are evil, bro, the guy advised sagely. Although he occupied the top bunk in their cell, leaving the bed below for Nate, he continued rambling. *No cap, bro. They're evil and, like, fuckin' criminal masterminds. I should have run fuckin' far away from Diamond when she came at me, bro . . .*

Nate tried to tune him out, focus on his thoughts, and think through his predicament. But he found he didn't much like the state of his own mind, and when lights out commenced, he allowed himself to float on the ebb and flow of sounds in the lockup. Some guys sobbed; others shouted gibberish; someone crooned a song in Spanish; another rapped; a lone, warbling voice chanted the Lord's Prayer.

Nate latched onto that prayerful inmate's voice and found a measure of peace as he whispered the familiar words along with him: *Our Father, who art in heaven, hallowed by thy name; thy kingdom come; thy will be done; in earth as it is in heaven. Give us this day our daily bread; and forgive us our trespasses as we forgive those who trespass against us; and lead us not into temptation, but deliver us from evil . . .*

42

———————

Nate posted bail the next morning.

As he paid the fee, he understood how fortunate he was to have the funds to free himself. From what he had overheard in the jail, plenty of his fellow inmates were flat broke and stuck pleading with family and friends to raise bail money.

But his circumstances were more precarious than ever. Another slipup like he'd had yesterday, and he could wind up in a predicament that couldn't be resolved by simply swiping a credit card.

Had Marvin gotten to Leslie? Did he show her the photos he'd snapped on his phone?

After the correctional officer returned his possessions and he dressed in his own clothes, the first thing he did was check his phone. He had a slew of messages from store employees and business associates; on a personal note, he had two messages from Danielle—a text and a voicemail.

But first, he called Leslie. She answered breathlessly before the ring completed.

"I'm out," he said.

"Thank God. Are you okay?"

"As okay as you could expect after spending a night in a smelly cell with a cellmate who wouldn't shut up."

"I'm coming to get you," she said. Then, in a tone that worried him: "We have a lot to talk about. Some things have happened since we spoke yesterday."

"What things, Les?"

"We'll get to that. I'm on my way."

Worried, he ended the call. He reviewed Danielle's messages; she was concerned about him, apologetic about Marvin's uninvited arrival at her house, and wanted him to call her as soon as he could.

He couldn't get entangled with her further, but the least he could do was let her know he'd been released. He sent her a brief text: "*I'm out on bail. Just waiting on my fiancée to pick me up. Thanks for your concern. Hope all is well.*"

She didn't respond, and she didn't call. Perhaps she had taken the hint. Despite their heavy flirtation yesterday and intense mutual attraction, they had no future. They needed to move on with their lives.

The afternoon temperature outdoors was in the low forties, so Nate hung out inside the jail complex until Leslie pinged him: "*Parked out front.*"

He zipped up his windbreaker and pushed through the glass doors. He saw Leslie's silver Honda parked outside at the curb, smoke puffing from the exhaust pipes.

He started forward.

"Nate!" a woman called out.

Nate pivoted to see Danielle striding across the parking lot, looking stylish in her jacket and boots, her braids swinging in the wind. He paused in mid-step as if the chilly breeze had flash-frozen him in place.

That sense of unreality that had earlier come over him returned. Looking at an approaching Danielle crossing in front of Leslie's sedan was like staring at alternate universes on a split screen: one woman was his future, and another was a future that might have been.

When Danielle touched his arm, he snapped back to the here-now.

"Hey," he said. "What're you doing here?"

"I had to make sure you were okay." Her big eyes looked moist. "And . . . I want to apologize to your fiancée for my brother and this entire fiasco. It's not like he will."

Never had Nate so strongly wished he possessed magical powers; he would have snapped his fingers and made Danielle disappear.

"It's not a good time," he said.

A door slammed. Leslie had climbed out of the car.

"You didn't do anything wrong," Danielle said. "Tell her the truth. I'll back you up."

Nate swallowed the lump in his throat. Leslie marched toward them. Her eyes were like scalpels.

He noticed a sheet of paper rippled in her gloved fingers.

"Who is this?" Leslie asked, gaze cutting from Danielle to Nate.

Before Nate could answer, Danielle jumped in.

"I'm Marvin's sister, Danielle," she said. "I'm here to apologize to you all for what my brother did."

Nate could see in Leslie's narrowed eyes that she was calculating Danielle's words.

"Why don't we go home, Les?" Nate said. "We can talk about all this later."

But as Leslie scanned Danielle from head to boots, her face morphed into a deep scowl. Nate felt his stomach clench.

"This is *her*," Leslie said. She thrust the paper she carried toward Nate, and her bladed gaze cut from Danielle to Nate. "Isn't it?"

Nate unfurled the sheet, the paper fluttering in the breeze. It was a sketch drawing, and he knew immediately that Marvin had created it. Marvin had used one of those infuriating photos he had taken yesterday as the basis for his piece: Nate and Danielle emerging from her front door, her hand on his arm. The eyes locked in soulful gazes. Looking like lovers after a fling.

Marvin strikes again, he thought, with a sinking feeling.

Beside him, Nate heard Danielle suck in a breath of surprise.

"You never told me where you were when you got arrested," Leslie said. She crossed her arms. "Were you with her, hmm?" She flicked her gaze at Danielle. "Marvin's sister?" She spat out the words as if they tasted sour.

"I went over there to put together a bookcase for her," Nate said, and the words poured out of him. "Marvin showed up when I was leaving and took a bunch of photos to make it look like I was doing something wrong—he knew you would flip out. I lost my cool and punched him, he called the cops, and I got arrested. But I was only doing her a favor, Les."

"You were doing her a favor," Leslie repeated. She scanned Danielle again, and her jaw tightened. "*This* woman?"

"He's telling the truth," Danielle said. "He's a good man. You're so lucky, girlfriend."

As Danielle finished her statement, she absently touched Nate's arm. Nate drew away from her, but Leslie's face screwed up into a deeper scowl.

"To hell with this." Leslie shook her head, her eyes glistening. "I can't . . . I've got to get out of here."

"Let's go home, babe," he said. "Let's talk it out."

Nate started to walk toward the car, but Leslie stuck out her arm.

"I can't be around you right now," she said.

"What? Come on, Les. I didn't do anything wrong!"

"He's telling the truth," Danielle said.

"I'm going to my family." Tears shimmering on her cheeks, Leslie hurried back to her car.

"Les, please!" Nate followed, but she locked the passenger door. "I love you. You know me!"

Leslie pulled away, exhaust fumes blowing into his face.

43

———————

Danielle offered to give him a lift back to her place so he could pick up his truck, but Nate declined.

"I need to be alone," Nate said. "I'll catch an Uber."

"I'm sorry." She sucked in her bottom lip. "Give Leslie time. She'll come around. She'll see you're telling the truth."

"She holds grudges. You have no idea."

Nate opened the Uber app on his phone and summoned a ride. The driver would arrive in twelve minutes.

"I can hang out with you until your Uber gets here," Danielle said. She hugged herself. "Want to wait in my car so we can get out of this cold?"

"I'll wait out here, alone. But thanks."

"All right, I'm heading back to work. I'll check on you later?" She hesitated. "Or how about you text me?"

"Yeah, whatever."

She hugged him and kissed his cheek before stepping away. He watched her stride across the parking lot and back to her car.

Nate looked at Marvin's drawing in his hand, the paper twisting and fluttering in the wind.

He found a nearby wastebasket and tossed the sketch in the trash.

<h1 style="text-align:center">44</h1>

The Uber driver wanted to chat with Nate about his presence at the Gwinnett County Jail. Nate realized how he must have looked: he was standing there with a worn bandage on his nose and tape wrapped around his knuckles from punching Marvin, awaiting a pickup outside the jail, appearing to the entire world like a recently released felon with a tale to tell. Nate answered the questions with curt responses, and the driver soon got the message and dialed up the radio's volume.

The issues facing him felt overwhelming. He was on the outs with Leslie. If she was going to stay with her parents, that meant her dad was undoubtedly coming soon to ask tough questions about his business investment, and new legal troubles simmered on the horizon.

And still, there was the Marvin Situation.

It's all my fault, he thought. He looked out the passenger window at the dreary, gray afternoon as the driver navigated metro Atlanta traffic. *Poor decisions landed me here.*

He should never have bailed out Marvin or hired him. Having lunch with Danielle and going to her house to assemble the bookcase had been a catastrophic blunder, too. His ill-considered choices had snowballed into his current predicament.

But he'd only wanted to do the right thing. That was what vexed him. It was his nature to help out, to see the best in people, to play the Good Samaritan or whatever. Yet his tendency to act like the good guy kept getting him in trouble.

On impulse, he called Leslie. She didn't answer, so he texted: "*I love you, baby. Please talk to me. You know me.*"

He saw the three little dots signaling her response, and then they vanished. He knew his fiancée; it would take her time to process everything. She was slow to forgive—and sometimes, she *didn't* forgive.

Nate closed his eyes and rested his head against the seat, pondering his next move.

But he'd gotten no sleep in the jail cell, and slumber came for him like a thief. He was surprised to snap awake and discover the driver turning onto Danielle's street. His truck waited at the curb in front of her duplex, where he'd left it parked.

"Drop me off up there behind the Chevy," Nate said.

"You got it, boss." The driver met his gaze in the rearview mirror. "Stay out of trouble, all right? I know it's tough out here in these streets, but we gotta keep our eyes on the prize, brother."

Everyone is a life coach these days, Nate thought. He grunted in reply and got out of the car. The driver sped off.

The biting wind had increased in ferocity, screeching out of the northwest. The temperature was in the low forties, which felt like subzero for an Atlanta native. Nate lowered his head and trudged toward his truck, but as he did, he absently scanned the duplex property—the scene of the crime, as it were.

Danielle's car was gone, as expected given her return to work. A white Toyota Highlander occupied the driveway, likely belonging to her neighbor. The SUV had been there yesterday, too, he remembered.

A cardboard box lay at the edge of the drive as if tossed there by a careless delivery driver. The sight irked Nate, given his livelihood in packing and shipping. He retrieved the box and checked the label.

It belonged to Danielle's neighbor. He carried it to the front door, placed it at the doorstep, and rang the doorbell. Without waiting for anyone to answer, he turned to leave.

He heard the door open behind him so quickly the person must have been watching him the entire time.

"Thank you, mister," a woman said.

Nate glanced over his shoulder and waved. "No problem."

"I saw the police nab you yesterday." The neighbor was an older Black woman. She wore a green hair bonnet, black sweatshirt, matching sweatpants, and white house slippers. "Lord, what a mess. All that screaming and shouting and carrying on."

Nate paused in his walk, shame burning his face. This lady reminded him of his mother. What was he going to tell Mom about this situation? He hadn't figured that out yet, either.

"I'm sorry for all the trouble," he said. "I know you were babysitting. I hope the boy wasn't too upset by what happened with his mom and uncle."

A frown creased the woman's face. "Who was babysitting?"

It was Nate's turn to frown.

"Danielle said her neighbor was babysitting her son," Nate said.

"You mean the pretty young lady who lives next to me?" The woman pointed with her thumb.

"Right. Her."

"She ain't got no children, honey."

Once again, a sense of the surreal came over Nate, like a cold hood.

"She doesn't have a son?" he asked.

"If she does, I ain't never seen him." The woman smacked her lips. "And I sure ain't done no babysitting for nobody."

Nate's heart slammed.

"Matter of fact, I only seen her and that man living there, the one you punched out." She snorted a laugh. "Boy probably deserved it, too. He acts crazy as a wood lizard."

She wriggled her fingers at him, scooped up her package, and disappeared inside.

Nate stood rooted in the icy wind. His blood felt about fifty degrees colder than the keening gale.

What in the hell was going on?

45

Shaken, Nate got in his truck, started the engine, and punched up the heat to the highest setting. Warm air enveloped him.

She ain't got no children, honey.

Nate had seen multiple photos of Danielle's son inside her house: a cute, brown-faced boy with an adorable smile. He hadn't imagined seeing those pictures. A lot had happened to him lately, but he sure hadn't taken a blow to the head.

Why would Danielle lie about it? Did she not have custody of the kid or something, and maybe wanted Nate to believe she did? Or was the kid pure fiction?

As much as she'd talked to Nate about the child, it seemed unfathomable that she had made up the boy's entire existence. Who did that? Why?

"It doesn't matter," Nate muttered to himself. "I'm not getting involved with her any further, anyway."

But it felt important, like unraveling the first outer layer of a big onion. It felt like something that might matter to Leslie, too, though he had no idea why she would care at this point.

He pulled away in his truck and started driving.

People from work had been blowing up his phone, but he first needed to get home and shower. Spending the night in the grimy jail made him feel like he'd been rolling in a pigpen.

He nursed a half-hearted hope that Leslie's car would be parked in the garage, but the bay was empty.

Empty for good? Have I lost my lady?

The thought was too heart-wrenching to contemplate.

He took a long shower. As he soaped and rinsed under the warm water, the neighbor's words haunted him: *She ain't got no children, honey.*

Marvin had remarked about his sister's child—his nephew—too, in a casual tone. There had to be a logical, simple explanation for all of this.

After showering, Nate dressed in fresh work clothes and picked up his phone from the nightstand in the bedroom, where he'd left it.

He had received a new text message. It came from Joseph Clark, Leslie's father, and contained only two words, which jolted Nate like a kick to the groin.

"Call me."

He didn't know what Leslie might have told her folks about the latest happenings, but an unforeseen, curt text message from her father was a bad sign.

"Shit," Nate said.

46

———

Nate didn't call Mr. Clark. He would eventually be forced to talk to the man but did not want to submit to an interrogation just then. First, he had to get things sorted out.

Whatever "sorted out" meant. He felt adrift, like a castaway clinging to a fragile raft in the deep ocean.

The only thing he *knew* he could do right then was go to work. "Rise and grind" had been his motto for years, and he found a measure of peace and purpose in work that few things could match.

He drove to his Norcross store. Denise gave him a pointed look when he entered.

"Look what the cat drug in," she said. "Is everything okay, boss? What happened to your hand?"

"I fell and scraped my knuckles. I'm fine."

"You fell?" Her upper lip wrinkled. "With all those bandages, you're starting to look like you went a few rounds with somebody and lost."

He liked Denise, but no way was he confiding that he'd gotten arrested for assaulting Marvin—though she may have wanted to hear that considering her dislike for the man—and spent the night in jail.

"I'll be in back." He started past her.

"When are we going to hire another clerk? We're getting smashed out here, boss."

On top of everything else he faced, he remembered that he needed to replace Marvin at the store.

Or you can call Marvin and ask him to return to work, Nate. You know, let bygones be bygones.

The idea was so ridiculous he chuckled, which brought a deeper scowl from Denise.

"I'm serious," she said.

"I'm working on it, Denise." *That and a million other things.*

"Your friend came by, too. Our former colleague."

"Marvin?"

She nodded. "He didn't come inside, thank God. But I saw him hanging around out front earlier today, like walking back and forth and smoking. When he saw me looking, the creep actually *winked* at me."

Nate's abraded knuckles tingled. If Marvin had been nearby, Nate might have slugged him again with that same hand.

"If you see him again, call the police and report him for trespassing," Nate said.

"What's going on between you guys? I feel like I'm stuck in the middle of something, and it's making me nervous. Is he going to start stalking me?"

Add another issue to the pile: Marvin harassing his employees. He could not afford to lose Denise.

"I'm sorry this happened," Nate said. "I'm taking care of it. I promise."

47

Later that evening, Nate visited his mother.

"What a nice surprise." Mom opened the door for him and welcomed him inside. Delicious aromas wafted into the entry hall, and Nate felt his stomach rumble. He realized he hadn't eaten anything all day. When stress overwhelmed him, he either devoured everything in sight or starved himself—there was no in between.

After he closed the store for the day, he'd texted Mom and asked if he could drop by. She responded: "*Sure. Is everything okay?*" To which he wrote only: "*See you soon.*"

He hugged her then, holding her for a beat longer than usual. She patted his back with her palm.

He finally let her go. She closed the door.

"Baby, what's wrong?" she asked.

"Am I a good man?"

"Of course you are." She glanced at his bandaged hand. "What happened?"

"Can I get something to eat, Mom? Please?"

She led him into the kitchen. For her dinner, she had prepared a large pot of homemade chicken soup. Although she lived alone, he knew she tended to still cook family-sized portions of meals out of long habit and would freeze the leftovers.

He sat across from his mother at the kitchen table, huddled over a steaming bowl sprinkled with oyster crackers, just like he would eat soup as a kid. Eating with the bandaged knuckles proved challenging, and soon, he gave up and held the spoon in his other hand.

Sipping iced tea, Mom watched him. She had to be eager to know the purpose of his unplanned visit, but she said nothing. Nate realized only two women in his life would have displayed that degree of patience with him—and the other one was refusing to speak to him just then.

"That was so good, thanks." Nate nudged aside the empty bowl. "I didn't realize how hungry I was."

"You haven't eaten today?"

Shaking his head, Nate took a long swallow of water. Mom folded her hands together on the table, but her gaze never left his face.

"What's going on?" she asked.

Mustering the courage to tell his mother the truth was tougher than coming clean with anyone else, including Leslie. He was forty-two years old, but facing his mom about this situation made him feel like a kid pressed to explain a failing grade on his report card.

"I spent the night in jail," he said.

Mom shut her eyes.

"Oh Lord," she said. Expelling a breath, she opened her eyes again. "This is about Marvin. Isn't it?"

"Marvin and his sister, Danielle."

"Danielle?" Mom straightened. "When did she come into the picture?"

"A lot's happened since we last spoke . . ."

In a halting voice, Nate told her everything, sparing few details.

Mom listened without asking questions, but when he shared the revelation about Danielle's son, her mouth opened wide as the bowl in front of him.

"Do you know if it's true?" Nate asked. "Does she have a son?"

"I haven't seen her since her mother's service. That was ten years ago. How old did she say her boy is?"

"Eight or nine?"

Mom tapped her lip as if summoning an old memory. "No, she wasn't pregnant back then that I could see. I would've remembered that. But why would she lie, Nate?"

"I feel like I'm missing something important." Nate took another gulp of water. "Do you know anyone who can verify it? Someone in her family?"

"I'll have to think on it. Nobody comes to mind. They have a tiny family, folks scattered here and there."

"But Leslie . . ." Nate lowered his head, feeling a heavy weight at the back of his neck. "She won't talk to me. I know how it looks from her side. Like I've cheated on her."

"Give her time, sweetheart." Mom reached for his hand. "Be honest with her, always. You don't have to remember a lie if you tell the truth."

"She's not the forgiving type, Mom."

"But she knows your heart. You believe in doing the right thing. She knows that about you, like I do."

"Yeah."

"That's why I want you to tell *me* the truth about something." With her hand still on his, Mom squeezed. "Why are you helping these two? Marvin, and now this thing with Danielle, going over to her house to do work and all? That's a lot of effort, even for you. Why?"

"Because I can." But Nate withdrew his hand from his mother's tightening grasp.

Mom crossed her arms over her bosom. "That's not an answer, Son."

"To whom much is given, much is expected. You taught me that. Remember?"

"*Why*, Nathaniel?"

Her penetrating, brown-eyed gaze punctured the very depths of his soul. Looking away from her, he stroked his beard-stubbled chin.

Tell your mother the truth.

"Thirty years ago," he started. "Things were bad with Marvin and his stepdad. As you know."

Mom watched him, but said nothing.

"Someone had to do something," he said.

Mom's mouth tightened. "And?"

"So I did something."

"What did you do?"

"I wrote an anonymous letter and slid it under the door of the principal's office," he said.

Mom bowed her head.

"Lord have mercy," she whispered.

"I guess the school called his parents, we saw Mr. Waters later when we were riding bikes, he rode up on us, so furious, he knocked the shit out of Marvin, grabbed him and took him back home, and Marvin, he was defending himself, you know? He was *defending himself*. But it was because of what I did, Mom. I only wanted to help. Someone had to do something. I had . . . I had good intentions, Mom. I meant well. I only wanted to do the right thing."

Nate felt his lip quivering, his eyes heavy with tears threatening to gush out of him. Mom covered her face with her hands, her petite frame shuddering. He got out of his chair, shuffled around the table to her, and went to put his arm on her narrow shoulders.

She shoved him away so hard he stumbled backward.

"Go," she said.

"What? Mom, come on. I'm sorry—"

"*Go!*"

Crying, she pointed toward the doorway with a trembling finger.

Nate opened his mouth, mumbled another lame, *I'm sorry*, and swallowed the rest of his words before he could say anything more and dig a deeper hole with his mother.

He saw himself out.

48

———

To Nate, his house felt emptier than ever, as if it belonged to someone else and he was only renting. The vacant rooms were caverns, and the hallways seemed vast, like long tunnels leading nowhere.

Everyone in his life that he cared about was upset with him. What had he done to deserve this abandonment except try to do the right thing?

No good deed goes unpunished. Now you know what that means, don't you?

Nate sat in his home office, opened his laptop, accessed his work email, and stared at the display. The letters on the screen might have been rendered in a foreign language. His brain felt unable to process them.

He clapped the computer's lid shut.

A framed photo of him and Leslie together at some work event stood on the corner of his desk. They looked like the prototypical power couple, smiling and dressed to impress.

He picked up his phone and called her.

He anticipated the phone would drop into voicemail oblivion, but after the second ring, she answered—but with silence.

"Les?" His throat felt as if it were clotted with glue. "Are you there?"

He heard soft breathing. It was how she sounded when lying beside him in bed late at night when it felt like they were the only two human beings in the world.

He licked his dry lips. He didn't have a speech planned and said only what popped into his thoughts.

"I miss you. I wish you were here."

He heard a catch in her breath.

"It's been a busy, crazy day," he said. "Marvin came by the Norcross shop when I wasn't there. He didn't go inside, but he stood out front like a weirdo stalker and winked at Denise. She's creeped out now, so I've got something else to deal with . . . and I went to see Mom. I told her everything. I finally told her about the letter. I can't believe I waited so long. I guess I knew she'd be mad at me, and man, you better believe she was. She kicked me out."

Lowering his head, Nate exhaled a deep, long breath. Leslie hadn't said a word, and he glanced at the phone to confirm the connection was still active, found that it was, and resumed talking.

"I found out Danielle doesn't have a kid," he said. When he heard a sharp intake of breath on the other end, he quickly said: "No, I didn't call her or go to see her, but when I went to pick up my truck, I ran into her neighbor, an older lady. She told me she's never seen her with a child, ever. So it seems like Danielle lied about that. I can't figure out why. Mom didn't know one way or the other. It feels important, maybe, to both of us. But I can't put my finger on exactly why it matters. It's bugging me."

He raked his fingers across his scalp and gazed at the shadowed ceiling.

The phone connection was still active, but he heard only Leslie's slow breathing.

"Did I already say that I miss you?" Nate said. "I want to marry you more than anything. Do you still want your big wedding? That's cool, but I want to marry you right away. I want to head over to the county courthouse and do it. That was something I've been meaning to tell you, Les. We could do it tomorrow, or soon, I hope. I hope and pray you can give me another chance. I love you."

Nate pulled his hand down his sweat-filmed face. "Goodnight, baby."

She didn't say a word.

But Nate heard a click on the other end as she disconnected the call.

49

The next morning, Nate discovered an email from his mother. She had sent it shortly after 4:00 a.m.

Nathaniel—

I'm still too upset to say this over the phone, so I'm sending you this message.

I'm extremely disappointed with what you told me last night. I know I warned you back then about meddling in that family's business.

But that was a long time ago—thirty years. You were only a child. I must remember that, too. I know you kept it from me because you knew I would disapprove. But you were only a young boy trying to help his friend. You went about it the wrong way, and things happened no one could have expected.

Let it go, and leave it in God's hands now, baby.

After you left last night, I called a couple of friends. They didn't know about Danielle's child, but her mother, Rachel, had a sister, a half-sister, actually. Did you know that? She moved into their house after Rachel and the kids moved out. The house stayed in the family.

Her name's Charlene Livingston. I never knew her well, but she might be someone you can talk to about this Danielle and Marvin business if you want. I don't have her number but I'm certain you still know the address. She may still live there.

    Love, Mom

50

Late that morning, Nate finally managed to leave his stores and drive across the metro area to his old Atlanta neighborhood, Summerhill.

He hadn't visited that section of the city since his mother had moved out of their house fifteen years ago. The old Turner Field, once the home of the Atlanta Braves, had been renamed and repurposed as a stadium for Georgia State University since the pro baseball team had exited for splashy new digs in the northern suburbs. As was happening all over the city, gentrification had swept through their former neighborhood. He saw breweries, indie restaurants, cafés, and trendy-looking shops—and plenty of folks who didn't resemble the regulars he had seen here when he was growing up, the new residents strolling the avenues sipping coffee and riding bicycles.

As the saying goes, the only constant was change.

He drove past their old home. The split-level house had been repainted, and a blue Subaru SUV bearing a Georgia Tech bumper sticker occupied the driveway. The surrounding sidewalks had also been repaved.

Out of curiosity, Nate had checked the property on one of those real estate estimate apps before heading over here. The house's projected value surpassed his own considerably larger residence in Lawrenceville.

Did anyone from back in the day still live here? Could they afford to?

He cruised a few blocks over to Marvin's childhood home. When had he last looked at it? Thirty years ago? He'd been afraid to lay his eyes on the place—the very idea of doing so summoned lurid memories from that awful day.

Marvin's house had been repainted, too; it was a cheery-looking pale yellow with black accents. A white Tesla was parked underneath the carport, and a red "Go Dawgs" yard sign stood in the front yard.

Marvin's relative no longer lived there, but Nate knew that before he had set out on his drive. Online, he found a record of a property sale two years ago. His mother's information about Marvin's aunt, Charlene Livingston, was out of date.

He swung his truck to the curb in front of the house next door, a white Craftsman with black shutters.

The neighbor's house hadn't been sold recently. It could still be in the hands of the same owner.

A ten-year-old silver Ford F-150 occupied the driveway; it had a "Disabled Veteran" license plate. The house was well-kept, not a shingle out of place. Whoever lived here cared about the property.

Nate had accepted that getting anything helpful from this visit was a long shot, but he was following his instincts. Danielle was lying to him, and he was convinced her deception was part of a broader plan and might connect somehow with Marvin, too. Her aunt had lived in their childhood home until recently; if she wasn't there, maybe her longtime neighbor could tell him something useful. Maybe.

Nate rang the doorbell.

He had taken care to wear his UPS jacket and ball cap. Anyone seeing him might assume he was a driver delivering a package and open the door.

A minute ticked by before the resident answered. It was a tall, gangly Black man with a well-groomed gray beard and a balding head; Nate pegged his age as early to mid-seventies. He wore denim overalls over a white button-down shirt and leaned on a gleaming wooden cane.

He assessed Nate with deep, cool brown eyes. Nate heard a television blaring behind him, the TV broadcasting some classic Western show like *Gunsmoke* from the sound of it.

"You got a package for me, son?" the man asked in a watery voice. He scratched his chin.

"Good morning, sir," Nate said. "My name's Nate Noble. I'm an old friend of the family who lived next door. Charlene Livingston is my friend's aunt."

The neighbor's eyes softened, and he let out a soft chuckle. "You're late, young man. Char moved out . . . what? Two years ago?"

"Oh, sorry to hear that."

"These folks *trying* to get rid of me, too. Hmph." He cast a sidelong glance at the homes behind Nate, and his face puckered into a frown. "But I ain't rollin' up out of here until the good Lord calls me home."

"So Miss Charlene moved away," Nate said, attempting to steer him back toward the point of his visit.

"You were friendly with that boy, Marvin?" the man asked.

This gentleman would answer questions in his own time, Nate realized.

"Marvin and I were best friends," Nate said. "But that was a long time ago."

"You know what that boy did, son? Don't you?"

Nate nodded.

"Damn shame what happened. A tragedy." The man shook his head, eyes downcast. "But I always said, it was gonna blow. Police getting called all the damn time 'cause of that ornery Negro, Leon. I was half a mind to take out my twelve-gauge and handle him myself."

Anger surfaced in his eyes. "He had it coming, that's what I say—only sorry the boy was the one to do it."

"So am I."

"But I knew he was gonna do it. Yes, sir. Sometimes, he'd come out there on the porch and just sit by himself for a long time—uh-huh. I was in 'Nam, son. Look on his face was familiar to me, yes, sir."

"Thanks for your service," Nate said.

But he went on as if Nate hadn't said anything.

"I know what it looks like when somebody got killin' on their mind. I've seen it up close. That boy was gonna take that fool out—and *nobody* was gonna stop him." He wagged his finger.

His words rang like a church bell in Nate's mind. *Nobody was gonna stop him.* Nate felt a slight easing of the tension in his shoulders.

What if none of this was his fault? What if Marvin was going to murder his stepfather regardless?

The possibility was so startling to Nate that it took him a moment to gather his thoughts.

"I lost touch with Marvin," Nate said. "I know his mom passed, too. I'm trying to reach his aunt."

The neighbor grunted. "Charlene moved into a home." He scratched his chin. "Windy Glade? Windy Hill? I wrote it down." He chuckled. "At my age, son, if you don't write everything down, you can't get by no more. Lemme go in the back and get it for you."

51

While Nate was talking to the neighbor, Denise sent him a text message and followed it up with a breathless voicemail.

"Mr. Clark is here, boss. You need to come right away."

One step forward and two steps back, Nate thought, climbing into his truck. He had neglected to call Leslie's father as requested yesterday, and Mr. Clark was not known for his patience. When he blew off Clark's text, he should have anticipated the man's follow-up visit to the Norcross store, but the issues in his world had besieged him like a hailstorm.

He messaged Denise: *"On my way. It's going to be at least forty-five minutes with traffic."*

"He says he'll wait," she responded.

Of course he will, Nate thought. *And he'll get angrier by the minute.*

He sped across town as fast as he dared, but his mind spun faster than the wheels of his truck. The talkative war veteran had given him a lead he could follow up on, and he was eager to see where it led. But he'd be a fool to ignore Leslie's dad any longer.

It took an entire hour to reach the Norcross store. As he screeched into the parking lot, he was hopeful that Mr. Clark's black S-Class Mercedes would be nowhere in sight, that the man would have lost his meager patience and gone elsewhere, but he noticed the distinctive sedan occupying a choice parking spot not far from the front door. The vanity license plate declared: JOEESQ.

Nate groaned and hurried inside. Denise headed him off as soon as he walked in. Her cheeks bloomed red as chili peppers.

"Please don't be mad at me," she said. "I was overruled, and I had customers to deal with. The guys are in the back."

"The guys, like plural? I thought it was only Clark?"

Nate heard distinctive laughter echoing from the rear of the store. A tremor passed through him.

It can't be.

"Sorry," Denise said.

He brushed past Denise, rounded the counter, and raced down the short corridor to the administrative area.

Marvin and Joseph Clark hung out in the small employee break room, chopping it up like old friends. Marvin wore the store uniform Nate had issued him, and he smoked a cigarette. Clark sat at the small round table, light glinting on his wire-rim glasses. Brown-skinned like his daughter, he was a short, broad-shouldered man clad in a navy-blue Armani suit; Nate had rarely seen the man outside his home wearing casual clothes. Clark had loosened his maroon tie, which was as relaxed as he allowed.

"At last, there you are, Nate," Clark said. Despite Clark's diminutive stature, he possessed a rousing baritone voice that could have rivaled the late actor James Earl Jones. Clark made a dramatic show of checking the time on his platinum Rolex. "Exactly *when* were you going to call me? Your childhood buddy here was filling me in on all the details you should have shared with me."

"You're slippin', bro," Marvin said in an exaggerated drawl. He puffed a cloud of smoke in Nate's direction.

"Excuse me for a moment, Joseph." Nate pivoted to Marvin and pointed at him. "I need you to get the hell out of here. I fired you."

"There you go, brother. You didn't officially let me go. We had a disagreement and a little scuffle, all right? Boys will be boys, like I was telling my man Joe here." Marvin winked at Clark. "Why don't we shake hands and move on?"

Marvin extended his hand toward Nate. Nate gaped at his hand in disbelief. If Clark hadn't been present, Nate would have clocked Marvin in the jaw again.

"You called the police on me," Nate said. "I spent a night in jail!"

"Aww, poor baby." Marvin's eyes glinted. "A night in jail never hurt anyone, Nathan. It makes you appreciate your freedom."

"Brother's got a point there." Clark nodded. "I spent a night in the can myself back in my youth. It straightened me out quick."

"Listen, this guy's a grifter," Nate said to Clark. "I don't know what lies he's been feeding you, but you can't believe anything he says."

Thick arms crossed over his chest, Clark's gaze shifted from Nate to Marvin, measuring, assessing.

"You promised me a partnership," Marvin said. "You're backing out of it. Now, who's the liar?"

"Joseph, this is nonsense. You don't know this guy. You *know* me."

"I used to believe I did," Clark said. "But your behavior lately has been deeply troubling, and I believe it's in my best interest to reconsider my commitments."

"Say it ain't so, Joe," Marvin said.

Nate was shaking. He started to reach for Marvin, to seize his collar and literally drag him out of the store, and he saw the amusement glimmering in Marvin's eyes and realized that was precisely what this psycho *wanted* him to do, to lose his composure again, in front of an audience. *It's what he does,* Danielle had warned him. Whatever she had confided about her own life notwithstanding, she had given him the truth about her brother.

Instead of reaching for Marvin, Nate dropped his hand to his waist and grabbed his phone from the holster clipped to his belt.

"I'm calling the police," Nate said. "I'm reporting you for trespassing."

"That's my cue, then." Marvin extinguished his cigarette on the counter. He mimed tipping a hat toward Clark. "It was a pleasure, sir. Let's do lunch sometime."

"We'll see, son." Clark watched Marvin, a scowl etched on his face, but the frown remained in place when he glanced in Nate's direction.

"Get the hell out of here," Nate said to Marvin. "Get out and never come back."

"We're not done, Nathan." Marvin sauntered into the hallway. "Not by half. You haven't paid your debt to me, and you know it."

"Get out!" Nate said.

From a couple of paces behind, he followed Marvin to the store's exit. Denise was assisting a customer with a package when Marvin whistled at her, and her face contorted with disgust.

He watched Marvin stroll across the parking lot and finally disappear amidst the parked vehicles.

Dragging his hand down his face, he headed back to face Clark.

"What do you owe that brother?" Clark asked, his bespectacled gaze as incisive as a laser. "As your primary investor, I'm entitled to some answers—and I want them now."

52

———

Leslie wasn't sure about this. Her emotions felt too raw, her heart too tender, for her to sit across the table from her fiancé at the restaurant.

But there she was.

"Thanks for coming, Les," Nate said again. "I've missed you something awful."

It was about 6:30 p.m. Nate had asked her to meet him for dinner at a cozy taqueria in Lawrenceville they frequented. The place featured flavorful margaritas and memorable food. Upon her arrival, she found Nate already there nursing a Coke, a basket of golden tortilla chips and a bowl of salsa verde waiting on the table.

He had stood and hugged her; to his credit, he didn't go in for a kiss. He had bags under his eyes and needed to shave, but he kept smiling as if pleasantly shocked that she had come.

Leslie was still sorting through her feelings. Did she truly believe Nate was cheating on her with Marvin's sister? When would he even have *time* for an affair? She'd always thought of him as too ambitious, and too focused, to get distracted by such trivial things. He didn't seem like those guys who said they were working or traveling for business, but actually were getting busy with a gaggle of side chicks; she had dated such men before, and there were always red flags if she dared to see them. Part of what she loved about Nate was the simplicity of his character. He was generous to a fault and committed to doing the right thing even when such actions came across as naive or risky. It was hard to view him as a basic, low-down cheater.

But . . . seeing that drawing Marvin had given her, and then encountering the woman in the flesh outside the prison, had stoked her jealousy. The woman was stunning, prettier than Leslie if she had to admit it, and Leslie felt some way about that, even though she knew full well that beauty ran only skin deep. Worse: Leslie recognized the desperate hunger in the woman's eyes when she looked upon Nate. This girl wanted Nate badly, and if she didn't already have him in her clutches, she was dead set on getting him. Nate admitted to spending time at her house to do some silly handyman thing, but claimed nothing had happened between them. Did she honestly believe that?

The server stopped by their table.

"Are you going to order the mango margarita, Les?" Nate asked. "Your fav?"

"Water for me, please," Leslie told the server.

The shine in Nate's eyes dimmed at her response, but she needed to keep a clear head. Alcohol could muddy her thoughts and lead her to say things she might regret later.

Nate picked up a tortilla chip and nudged the basket toward her, but she didn't reach for it.

"I'm doing low carb, remember?" she said.

"Oh yeah, so you can fit into the dress on the Big Day?"

She saw hope sparkle in his eyes and felt her heart thaw a few degrees. But she didn't want to discuss the wedding.

The server stopped by again with a glass of ice water for her and asked if they were ready to order. Leslie hadn't bothered to peruse the menu and requested her usual taco salad with grilled chicken, while Nate asked for a burrito.

"You said you had something to discuss?" she asked Nate.

"Right." He knotted his hands on the table. "It's about the Marvin Situation, of course."

"Who else?" She massaged her temple; she already felt a new stress headache coming on. "Now what?"

"He showed up today at the Norcross store, this time when your dad had dropped in. Marvin was still wearing his uniform, so they got to talking. The next thing I know, when I get back after an errand, they're chatting in the back like best buddies. Marvin's lying shamelessly to him about our relationship, saying all kinds of craziness about being my new partner, whatever. I kicked Marvin out, but after that, your dad grilled me *hard*."

"What did you expect, Nate? Dad's got a lot riding on his investment with you. All I said to my parents about this entire situation was that you'd gotten into a fight and spent the night in jail, and Dad got agitated."

"Why did you tell him about that? I asked you not to say anything."

"You lost that privilege when I saw that woman of yours outside the jail."

He blew out an exasperated sigh. "I told you, nothing is going on between us."

She measured his expression, looking for signs of a lie or nervousness. His eyebrow usually twitched when he was stressed, but that wasn't happening here. He had either mastered the poker face, or he was telling the truth.

"Now your dad's thinking about putting his funding on pause." Nate dragged his hand down his chin and lowered his gaze.

"I hope you're not asking me to talk him out of it," she said. "Because, as I've told you many times before, I'm not getting involved in your business with my dad. My name is Paul, and that's between y'all."

"I need to get rid of Marvin." Nate placed his palms flat on the table and gave her a direct look.

"Get rid of him? What does that mean? You make it sound like you're going to hire a hit man."

Nate laughed. "Is that an option?"

Leslie smiled, and for a moment, everything was normal between them again, the two of them putting their heads together to solve a problem and sharing laughter at life's absurdities.

"I'm thinking of paying him to go away," Nate said.

"Paying him? You can't be serious."

"He wants me to buy him a new car. He said that the first time we nearly got into a brawl a few days ago, that I should replace his rust bucket with a new ride."

"That's like rewarding a child for bad behavior."

Nate's brows furrowed. "I'm not talking about a Benz or anything like that. It doesn't need to be brand-new, only better than the hoopty he's driving today."

"What you *need* to get is a restraining order," she said. "They'll throw his crazy ass in jail if he comes around again."

"They threw *my* ass in jail for assaulting him. He'd have an easier time getting a protective order against me."

Despite her earlier refusal, Leslie reached for the tortilla chips, dipped a couple of them in the salsa, and devoured them. Stress eating, perhaps, but she couldn't resist.

"I don't agree with this at all," she said. "And please, don't start again with that *you owe him* crap. You don't owe him a damn thing. You've gone above and beyond with Marvin on several fronts."

"I know you're right." Nate blew out a deep breath. "I only want to go back to how things were, Les, for the both of us. I'm worn out from all this drama."

"Get the restraining order. Don't wait for another incident. Just do it."

He grimaced, as if her suggestion pained him.

"Taking out a restraining order against a guy I grew up with feels wrong," he said. "I've never done something like that before."

Leslie started to argue, but Nate raised his hand.

"I'll have to get over it," he said. "You're right. It's going to be messy because I've got this ridiculous assault charge to deal with, but that's how lawyers earn their money, huh?"

She smiled at him and squeezed his hand. "You know what? I *do* want that margarita now—the skinny version. I feel like I've finally got something to celebrate."

Nate didn't look as happy as she felt, but he raised his glass. "Cheers."

53

Outside in the restaurant parking lot, Nate watched Leslie drive away, her vehicle's taillights dwindling in the dusk.

He'd asked her if she was coming home soon, and she only said, *I need time.* He needed to accept that answer, as much as it pained him. But their dinner felt like a turn in the right direction. She was still wearing her engagement ring. They initially disagreed with his strategy for handling Marvin, but he had come around to her point of view, and it was a civil discussion. There was hope for them.

Don't blow it, Nate.

He got in his truck and called Marvin before he lost his nerve. He made sure to use the app he'd installed on his phone to record the conversation, a suggestion Leslie had given him to gather evidence that might be useful later.

Marvin answered so quickly that Nate wondered if he was anticipating the call.

"Nate dawg." Marvin chuckled. "How'd things go with future father-in-law, huh? Is he down with me joining the partnership?"

"Here's the deal," Nate said. "I don't ever want to see you again."

Marvin paused for so long that Nate worried he had hung up. It sounded as if he had put his hand over the speaker to muffle a voice in the background.

"Are you trying to threaten me, man?" Marvin asked.

"This is how it's gonna be, Marvin: You stay away from me, Leslie, everyone in our lives. You stay away from my stores. No visits, no contact whatsoever, ever again. That's the deal."

"Or what? What're you gonna do, Nathan, if I don't follow your rules?"

Nate squeezed the phone, his pulse throbbing in his temple. "Don't try me."

"Do you think a restraining order scares me, bro?" Marvin asked. "I know Danny's bigmouthed ass told you all about my record."

Nate clenched his teeth. "I have nothing else to say to you, Marvin."

"Considering all we've been through, it's kind of hurtful to me, you trying to cut me off like this. Remember those bike rides and gaming sessions, brother?"

"Just stay away."

Nate terminated the call. He exhaled a pent-up breath, but it failed to ease the tension tightening like steel coils across his chest.

The app had recorded the call, but fresh doubts had crept into his mind. How far was Marvin going to push this? Was an order of protection worth the weight of the paper on which it would be printed? Nate had read plenty of news stories of stalkers who had orders slapped on them, and they still made life a living hell for their targets. It was only a deterrent, and it might have no impact on a reckless felon like Marvin.

After several aimless minutes of imagining how this might play out, Nate started the engine. His phone beeped.

He thought it might be Marvin calling back already to taunt him —but it was Danielle. Nate had no intention of ever communicating with the woman again, but since she had called, he could also take this opportunity to clear the air with her.

"Hey," he said.

"Whoa, you don't sound too happy. I know I was supposed to wait for you to call me, but I was worried about you. Is this a bad time?"

"There's been nothing but bad times since I reconnected with your pain-in-the-ass brother."

"Oh Lord." She made a *tsk-tsk* sound. "What did he do now?"

"It doesn't matter, Danielle. But I need you to come clean with me on something, on general principle."

"Okay." He heard hesitation in her tone.

"When I picked up my truck from your place yesterday, I ran into your neighbor at the duplex, a very sweet older lady. She said she's never babysat for you. She said she's never seen you with a kid, ever. What's the deal? Why'd you lie?"

Danielle didn't immediately respond. Nate heard only the soft rumble of the truck's engine and the hum of heat blowing from the air vents.

Although the call was still active, he asked, "Are you there?"

He heard a stifled sob.

"I'm so sorry," she said in a tremulous voice. "I'm sorry I lied. The truth . . . it's pathetic."

"I'm listening."

As he tapped the steering wheel, he heard her choking back tears.

"I lost custody of my baby to his father . . . to his *rich* daddy," she said with a touch of venom in her tone. Her voice softened. "I was ashamed to tell you. I didn't want you to see me as a horrible mother."

It wasn't the answer Nate had expected. Actually, he wasn't sure what he had expected, but it certainly hadn't been *that*. So much for the great mystery he assumed had been swirling around him.

"You didn't need to lie to me," he said. "I wouldn't have judged you."

"Oh, really, Nate? Your mom raised you and your sister on her own. She's a queen in your eyes. And then you'd look at me and know I lost custody of my baby boy."

"It doesn't matter what I think about your situation."

"It matters to *me* what you think. I should have told you the truth from the beginning. I'm so sorry you had to find out that way."

Although she sounded sincere, he questioned her integrity. What type of person created such an elaborate web of deceit about their child?

And what else had she lied about?

She and Marvin aren't that different, he realized. *They're both trying to hustle me—she's just a lot smoother about it.*

"Can you please forgive me?" she asked. "I'll make it up to you, sweetie, if you give me a chance."

"It's cool, Danielle." The shift in the conversation made him wary. He didn't want to give her false hope about the possibility of them ever amounting to anything. "Listen, I—"

"Is your fiancée back home with you?" she asked. "Or is she still upset?"

"We're working things out."

"So that's a no."

"She needs time." He ought to stop explaining the situation to Danielle, but she was easy to talk to—a big part of what had landed him in trouble in the first place.

"I see." Danielle's voice downshifted to a velvety note. "Can I come over? Sounds like we could use each other's company tonight."

If he had been younger and steeped in the intoxicating influence of hormones, he would have disregarded her lies and accepted her offer without question. A night with her promised to be pure erotic bliss, leaving him with tingly memories that would stay with him for years.

But he was forty-two, a grown-ass man. He wasn't perfect, but he knew himself well enough to understand it was well past time to stop the other head from making his decisions.

"That's not a good idea," he said.

"You hesitated." She let out a ripple of soft laughter.

"It's probably best if we stop communicating."

"*Probably?* Baby, admit you can't stop thinking about me, hmm? I'll admit that I can't stop thinking about you."

"I'm sorry, but I've gotta go. You take care, Danielle."

Nate ended the call without giving her a chance to respond. He rubbed his hands together. Sweat slicked his palms, and the truck's interior suddenly felt as muggy as a steam room. He dialed down the heat and lowered the window a few inches to let cold air pour inside.

After he finally cooled off, he drove home.

The house felt emptier than ever, like an abandoned fortress on a remote mountaintop.

54

———————

Danielle's hand trembled as she put down the phone after calling Nate.

"You have no idea how much you've screwed this up for us," she said. With as much sarcasm as she could manage, she added: "*Brother.*"

He sat on the sofa in her place playing a video game, but she knew he had been eavesdropping on her call with Nate.

"You had your chance to seal the deal, too, *sis*," he said.

She strutted past him and into the bedroom. He got up and followed, pausing in the doorway.

She snatched open the closet door and thumbed through outfits with her manicured fingers.

"Where are you going?" he asked.

"I need to throw on something sexy and get to Nate's. He's all alone tonight. I won't get another chance like this."

"Can I come with?" His voice was uncharacteristically meek.

"You know damn well he doesn't want to see you. He just told you that!"

"But it might be my last chance, too. We're still in this together, Danny. Right?"

Danielle shot him a harsh look. Why had she ever agreed to run this game with him? In the truest sense of the word, he was a mess—disorganized, volatile, short-sighted. The plan had been simple: take Nate Noble, Marvin's childhood best friend, for as much money as they could squeeze out of him. She had her ways of doing that, and he had his, too. But while she had been executing her side of things (with the unfortunate exception of Nate's discovery about her son), he had been causing unnecessary problems and antagonizing Nate and his woman.

Like attacking the grocery store guy, punching Nate in the face, and getting tossed into jail. Just . . . why? Or that silly incident with him showing up at her place to snap pictures when she had Nate there. None of those actions were based on their plans—it was all him, behaving erratically. His assignment was to get a job at Nate's store, then gain Nate's trust and access to his finances, and it had been an utter trainwreck.

He had lost his touch. She didn't know what had happened to him to make him so incompetent, but living your life on the edge sometimes could send you teetering *over* the edge, and you might never find your way back.

"Please, Danny," he said, in a whiny voice that she loathed. "I need this. You know I do."

He was desperate, that was obvious. She supposed she owed him —he *had* tipped her off to Mr. Nate Noble in the first place, after Nate came through his check-out line at the supermarket. Upon finding out that Nate owned not one, but three UPS stores and lived in a big house, Danielle knew they had found a mark worth their time.

Also: who was a more deserving target than Nate? The guy played a role in destroying her family thirty years ago. It didn't matter to her that Nate was a kid back then—his actions were consequential, and he deserved some pain and suffering.

God knows, she had suffered plenty since the dissolution of her family. Life had long been tough for her. As a grown woman, she had her good looks, but beautiful women were a dime a dozen, especially in Atlanta, a city full of sexy starlets and gorgeous grifters. In her opinion, you needed more than a cute face, tiny waist, nice boobs, and a big booty to get ahead these days: you needed a hustle. Something that could benefit you for years after your hotness had faded.

Don't waste the pretty, Mama had used to say. Her late mother had been a bona fide bitch, and Danielle was glad she was dead, but her words of wisdom hadn't been lost on her daughter.

If she played this right, Mr. Noble could be her dependable annuity plan for the next eighteen years.

"Please, Danny?" he said, again.

Danielle sighed. He had brought her Nate; she could throw him a bone, for old time's sake.

"You'll have to stay out of my way," she said. "In other words, I wrap up first—then I'm out and he's all yours. Can you handle that?"

He bobbed his head. "Yeah. Do your thing."

"Be ready in ten minutes. We've gotta move."

He grinned at her.

Danielle gave him a little smile, but she promised herself: when this job was done, she was done with him, for good.

55

———

Nate had been home only twenty minutes or so when someone rang the doorbell. He opened the doorbell camera app on his phone—and frowned.

It was Danielle.

She wore a black wool pea coat, her braids down and flowing to her shoulders. As he watched, she flicked a strand of hair away from her face, moved forward, and rapped on the door.

Nate was in his office reviewing work emails and sipping a nonalcoholic beer. But his thoughts had been unsettled, the faces of Leslie, Marvin, and Danielle bobbing and weaving in his mind's eye like unfettered balloons, each one weighted with worrisome thoughts. He missed Leslie; Marvin had yet to get back in touch with him; and Danielle only confused him.

Danielle knocked again. He bounded out of his chair and rushed into the hallway.

He opened the door, but only a few inches. Cold air poured inside through the gap, blowing the intoxicating scent of her fragrance into his face.

She wore light makeup as usual, but her eyes looked glassy as if she had just wiped away fresh tears.

"What the *hell* are you doing here?" he asked.

She edged to the doorway's threshold. She stood so near he felt the warmth emanating from her body.

Although her pea coat was buttoned, he saw that, underneath, she wore a satiny red blouse that revealed a smooth curve of flesh and a gold necklace with a heart-shaped pendant hanging amidst her cleavage.

It was easy—far too easy—to allow her beauty to mesmerize him. She was almost irresistible. Almost.

"Marvin told me where you lived," she said. "I'm sorry, I know you told me not to come over, but I hated how things ended with us, with you dismissing me as some lying skank."

"You can't be here. You need to go home."

She ran her tongue across her glossy lips. He remembered how soft those lips had felt when pressed against his, the moistness of her skilled tongue.

Get her out of here, man. Now.

"Can I come in?" she asked. "Please?"

She put one hand on the front of his shirt, her delicate fingers tracing across his chest; she slipped her other hand around his waist.

Her big eyes glistened.

"I'm sorry," he said. "No, you can't come in. You need to go."

He started to pry her hands off him. He felt a stinging sensation on his right side, where she had placed one of her hands.

A couple of years ago, Nate had been severely dehydrated due to a nasty stomach bug; his blood pressure had dropped to dangerous levels, and he had passed out on the kitchen floor, though fortunately, Leslie was there to revive him and summon medical assistance. The dizziness and weakness that swept over him just then felt like that health crisis.

He stumbled, his legs wobbly as crumbling pillars.

"Sweetie?" Danielle stepped inside. "What's wrong?"

The world spun like a nightmarish roulette wheel.

"*Help . . .*" Nate gasped.

He felt himself falling and groped for something to stop him, but his grasping hands found no support.

Chased by the haunting echoes of a familiar laugh, he plummeted into darkness.

56

When Leslie pulled into the driveway of her parents' house in Brookhaven, she messaged Nate, as she'd promised before they parted ways at the restaurant. He didn't respond.

"Text me when you get to your parents' and let me know you made it," he had said. It was a small thing, an innocent check-in, and she was only doing what he had asked. They'd had a pleasant dinner, so letting him know she had arrived safely was the least she could do.

She expected a swift reply, but she heard nothing.

Under normal circumstances, she would have shrugged it off, gone into the house, and hung out with her family for the rest of the evening. But nothing had been normal for them lately.

She called Nate. He didn't pick up. Worry threaded through her chest.

I'm probably overreacting, she thought.

She sat in her Honda sedan holding the phone in her lap, the car's engine thrumming.

She missed Nate, obviously. They were going through a rough patch as couples sometimes did, and though she nurtured a growing optimism that everything would work out, she had thought spending another night apart might be good for them—good for her, anyway, as she needed to be clear on her feelings and motivations in this relationship. Fear of missing out on her Big Day wasn't a sufficient reason to stand by him. She had a couple of girlfriends who'd done such a thing: married a man they weren't committed to merely because they wanted a wedding, and within a year, wound up divorced and bitter.

She missed the sound of his voice, the smell of him when she lay next to him in bed at night, that sense of deep comfort that enveloped her when he held her in his arms.

But this sudden concern of hers had nothing to do with missing him. It felt like intuition. A warning.

Something's wrong.

Leslie had experienced such feelings before. She had a profound emotional bond with her mother. Last year, Mom suffered a heart attack—a minor one, thank the Lord, but bad enough to land her in the hospital. Around the time it happened, Leslie had been at work in a meeting, and a sensation of sheer distress had come over her, her mother's face flashing like a beacon in her mind. Leslie had excused herself from the meeting and called her parents' home. Dad answered in a shell-shocked tone, *"I was just about to call you, sweetheart. The paramedics are coming for your mom . . ."*

Leslie called Nate again.

Once again, the phone rang several times and dropped into voicemail.

It was only about half past eight. He would be working in his home office, probably sipping a nonalcoholic beer, and after a while, he would go upstairs, read a business book for a bit, and turn in around eleven. He was such a creature of habit that you could set your clock by him.

She called him a third time.

Still, no answer.

She opened the Ring app on her phone. The cameras were dark

and inactive. According to the status icon, the video monitoring system was offline due to an internet outage.

That had happened before, but it was unusual—and something Marvin had said surfaced in her mind.

You know, I could cut your internet, make that little camera you love go dark and have some fun with you . . .

Was she being paranoid? In her current state, anything unexpected felt significant and troubling.

She needed to be sure.

Leslie texted: "*I'm coming home. Be there soon. Call me when you get this message, please. I'm worried.*"

57

———

Nate awoke and had no idea where he was. The world was blurred as if viewed through a soapy window. The back of his head ached, and his mouth tasted like a litter box.

He raised his left arm. His limb felt heavy, and it obeyed sluggishly as if a sputtering connection existed between his brain and body.

Groaning, he dragged his left hand across his eyes. The effect was that of wiping a foggy glass clear with a towel.

He was lying on the sofa in his house's family room. Danielle sat beside him, crouched over him like a nurse checking his vitals. She wore an unbuttoned coat and a skimpy red blouse underneath.

What was *she* doing here? His recollection of what had been happening before was fuzzy.

"Hey," he said. His mouth felt packed with gravel.

"Thank God, you're finally awake." She touched his cheek. "You tripped and hit your head, sweetie. I was so worried."

"What . . . what are you doing here?"

"I was a naughty girl." Clasping her hands in her lap, she gave him a mock-pouting expression. "You didn't ask me to come over, but I did. My brother gave me your address."

The mention of her brother, Marvin, kindled a spark in his memory. Nate started to sit up. The movement sent a rivet of pain corkscrewing through his head that made him hiss.

"Take it easy," Danielle said. "You hit your head hard. You might have a concussion."

Gingerly, he touched the back of his skull, where it pulsed the most painfully. He felt a tender bump.

With a wince, he craned his neck and took in his surroundings. His mobile phone lay on the coffee table, next to a red leather satchel he assumed belonged to Danielle; a plastic baggie peeked from the corner of the bag's mouth.

He also saw an ice pack from his freezer sitting on a coaster on the same table, beside a roll of toilet paper.

The oversized decorative clock above the fireplace mantel read ten minutes to nine. How long had he been knocked out?

But there was a more pressing question to which he needed an answer.

"Is Marvin here?" he asked.

"Marvin?" Giggling, Danielle touched his face again. "Aww, baby, you're so confused. Why would I bring Marvin with me when I wanted you all to myself?"

"I heard him laughing. Right before I blacked out."

"You must have been dreaming, sweetie. It's only the two of us, and now that you're up, I need to get going. Your fiancée is coming home."

"Huh? How do you know that?"

"She texted you, silly." Danielle picked up his phone and passed it to him.

Nate saw Leslie had texted him about twenty minutes ago to let him know she had arrived at her parents, and then she called three times, and followed up with another text: "*I'm coming home. Be there soon. Call me when you get this message, please. I'm worried.*"

Danielle rose from the sofa.

"How long was I knocked out?" he asked.

"Hmm." Danielle screwed up her face as if thinking. "Only a few minutes."

"Only a few minutes?"

"Uh-huh." Danielle buttoned her coat. "It's too bad, you hitting your head and now your lady coming back. We could've had a little fun, you and I. Bad timing, huh?"

As he sat up all the way, Nate felt a faint but distinct prickle of discomfort on his right side. Another piece of memory tumbled into place like a domino.

"You injected me with something," he said. "You drugged me."

She wrinkled her nose. "Drugged you? Don't be ridiculous."

But Nate dimly remembered: Danielle worked as a medical assistant, right? She might've had access to sedatives and would have known how to administer an injection stealthily.

His accusation wasn't ridiculous at all.

He pushed to his feet. The sudden movement threatened to spill him over, and he grabbed the sofa to keep from falling, yet he still felt woozy.

"Be careful there," Danielle said. "You should sit, hmm?"

He ignored her. He noticed his pants hung low on his waist and checked his leather belt. It was fastened on the wrong notch.

He became aware of a dull soreness in his groin, too.

"What did you do to me?" he asked.

"Lie back down and get some rest, baby." She swung her purse strap across her shoulder. "Can I get a smooch before I go?"

She quick-stepped to him before he could react, grabbed the front of his shirt, and tugged him toward her. He raised his hands to shove her away. She gave him a sloppy kiss that left lipstick smeared across his mouth.

"Get out!" he said.

As he tried to push her, she evaded him, and he lost his balance and collapsed to the rug on his knees. The world tilted, and nausea clutched his stomach.

"We'll see each other again soon." She giggled, backing away. "In family court, daddy."

Family court? Jesus, what did she do to me?

He tried to rise, but in his drug-addled state, he lost his balance again and spilled across the floor.

Danielle hurried out of the room, heels clicking against the hardwood floor in the hallway. He heard the connecting door to the garage open and slam shut. A few seconds later, he recognized the familiar sound of the sectional garage door opening.

With great effort, he pushed upward and fumbled for his phone to call Leslie, but his earlier fear returned.

I know I heard Marvin laughing. What if he's still in the house?

58

Leslie swerved onto their residential block. Their house stood ahead at the end of the cul-de-sac. She didn't see any vehicles in the driveway—expected since Nate usually parked his truck in the garage—but light glowed in one of the front windows on the lower level, the room where he kept his office.

It was not a reassuring sight. That shimmering light meant Nate was likely home but hadn't responded to her messages.

This behavior was totally out of character for him. What was going on?

As she neared the driveway, the garage door scrolled upward. She hadn't yet touched the remote door opener clipped to her sun visor.

In the light streaming from the garage's ceiling, Leslie saw an unfamiliar black Honda Civic parked alongside Nate's Chevy, in *her* vehicle's normal spot. A woman she recognized sashayed to the Honda, wearing a long coat and heels.

Danielle.

"You've gotta be kidding me," Leslie said. She tightened her grip on the steering wheel.

Barely two hours ago, Nate had been sitting across from her in the restaurant with apparently earnest eyes. Now he'd come home to host this skank?

It didn't make any sense. Was this what her intuition had warned her about? It would explain why he hadn't responded to her messages, wouldn't it?

She could have turned around then and returned to her parents' place for good. Driven away and out of Nate's life forever. What more did she need to see? Nate was a liar and a cheat, and if he wanted this homewrecker, he could have her. She wasn't going to compete with another woman for *any* man.

As Danielle reached for the car door, she looked up and noticed Leslie at the end of the driveway. The bitch waved at Leslie like they were old friends.

"Oh, hell no," Leslie said.

Leslie slammed into Park, ripped off her seat belt, and kicked open her door so quickly the hinges squealed.

"Hey!" Leslie stomped across the driveway, arms swinging, hands clenched into fists. "Get back here, bitch!"

Danielle scrambled inside her car and revved the engine. As Leslie reached the garage, the Honda roared backward, and if Leslie hadn't dodged to the left, the woman would have mowed her down.

Passing by, Danielle flipped Leslie the bird.

Shaking with rage, Leslie looked around for something, saw a small paver stone at the edge of the flower bed, and snatched it up and heaved it at the Honda like an Olympian performing a shot put.

The paver smashed against Danielle's windshield, leaving a spiderweb of cracks, and dropped onto the driveway. Danielle barely avoided hitting Leslie's sedan. She cut the wheel sharply and roared out of the cul-de-sac.

"Bitch!" Leslie shrieked at the departing car.

You've lost your damn mind, girl. Calm down.

She was panting, her palms scraped from grabbing and hurling that stone. But this wasn't over yet.

She still had to deal with Nate, her so-called fiancé. He wasn't getting away with this. This was all his fault, and she would blast him with the full effect of her fury before she left him for good.

She marched to the connecting door and flung it open.

59

———

Drawing measured breaths to steady himself, Nate had settled back onto the sofa to call Leslie when he heard a violent commotion outside: screaming, a crashing noise that sounded like glass crunching, screeching tires. Despite his brain fog, he realized it must be another mess unfolding, and from its sounds, the conflict was between Leslie and Danielle.

Could the timing of Leslie's arrival be any worse?

He needed to step outdoors and see what was happening, but first, he had to get his legs under him. As he gathered his bearings, Leslie stormed inside the house like a category-five cyclone.

An emotion surpassing fury flashed in her eyes. He'd seen her angry before, but never in a state like this. Eyes dilated, glistening with tears. Hair wild. Lips peeled back from her teeth like a feline predator ready to rip something apart.

She pointed at him and shrieked in a tone that punctured his eardrums: "You! You goddamn liar!"

"Les . . ." Nate wetted his parched lips with a tongue that felt as dry as cardboard. "It's not whatever you think it is."

"How could you?" Leslie cried, trembling. "Huh? After everything you said tonight? How could you turn around and do this to me, you bastard?"

"Listen to me. Please. I can explain."

She tore off her engagement ring and hurled it at him. The diamond pelted him in the face like a shard of glass. Wincing, he picked up the ring and placed it on the table.

"I'm so done," she said. "You did this to us, it's all on you, and I'm not here for it anymore."

He heard the finality in her tone. Was it even worth the effort to explain what had happened? Was she lost to him forever?

If so, he probably deserved it. None of what had happened was her fault, and if she hadn't been tied up with him, none of this chaos would have been visited upon her.

But he couldn't let her go without speaking his piece.

"I'm truly sorry for everything I've put you through," he said. "If you want to walk out on me forever, Les, I'll understand. I've made some terrible decisions—I know that. I take full responsibility for them. Always trying so hard to be the nice guy, you know? Mr. Good Intentions. But it's gotten me into trouble and dragged you down into the gutter with me, too. I hope you can forgive me, but I under- stand if you can't." Sighing, he fingered the throbbing knot on his skull. "I'm being one hundred percent honest when I tell you that she drugged me. That's how she got in."

"What?" She blinked at him in obvious bewilderment. "Who did what?"

"Danielle—I never asked her to come over. She showed up, I opened the door and told her to leave. She jabbed me with a needle, I guess. I passed out, banged my head." He released a heavy sigh. "I don't know what she did while I was blacked out. Before she left, she said something like, 'See you in family court, daddy.'"

"Family court? What the hell does that mean?"

"I'm not sure." He had suspicions, but what he'd told Leslie already sounded so outlandish he didn't dare go any further.

"None of that makes any sense, Nate." Glaring at him, Leslie balled her fists on her waist. "Not a single word of it. You're lying again and you sound like a damn fool."

"I think Marvin came in with her. I heard him laughing, right before I fell."

"Jesus, you sound ridiculous now." Leslie shook her head. "Did you fall and hit your head or what?"

"I did hit my head—that's what I just said, Les." He held her gaze. "But I *know* what I heard. Did you see Marvin leaving with her?"

"The bitch damn near ran me over."

"Was Marvin with her or not?"

"*No!* What the hell's the matter with you? Why would Marvin be with her? Why would you suggest that nonsense?"

Nate pulled in a slow breath and rose from the sofa. "Then I need to search the house."

"You're serious." Some of the anger had faded from her voice, replaced by confusion. "You really believe he's here?"

"Will you help me look around? Please?"

"Whatever, fine." She snatched her hair away from her face. "Then I'm gone."

"Fair enough." He started toward the hallway, taking care of where he put his footsteps. The sedative mostly had worn off now, but a lingering fuzziness outlined the edges of his awareness, and his stomach convulsed as if he might vomit.

Leslie must have noticed his trepidation. She laid a steadying hand on his arm, and she seemed to regard him with fresh, clear eyes.

"You're telling the truth, aren't you?" she said. But it didn't sound like a question.

"It's a crazy time." He nodded. "Yeah. I'm not lying."

"I'm struggling to process this." She pressed her fingers against her temple as if thinking about these things was excruciating. "None of it makes any sense."

"Let's finish looking around, and then we can talk."

Together, they searched the house, starting with his office. Nate immediately recognized that someone had rifled through his things: a file cabinet drawer was half-open, the numerous folders thumbed through; a notepad had been moved; and a Mason jar of pens was tipped over. But a quick check confirmed that nothing was missing.

Searching the rest of their home yielded similar results. Items had been disturbed from their usual spots, but nothing had been taken. They kept a heavy, fireproof safe nestled deep in the master bedroom's walk-in closet behind a screen of Leslie's old dresses, and those outfits had been tossed to the floor during a frantic search. The safe contained a pistol, a few thousand in cash, and jewelry; nothing had been taken. Opening the safe required a fingerprint or a five-digit PIN, and Danielle couldn't have supplied either.

After they finished looking, they returned downstairs.

"He's not here," Leslie said. "Someone tossed through our stuff, and it was probably her." Leslie sucked her teeth. "The shady-ass bitch."

"I must have imagined hearing Marvin," he said, but he was reluctant to admit that possibility.

"We need to call the police and report what she did. They'll arrest her ass."

"Do you think the cops will believe me? It's a crazy story."

"We make the report, Nate. We need to handle this situation the right way. It's not the time to go off in left field with silly ideas like offering to give Marvin a damn car."

Nate bit his tongue against a comeback. Probably, he'd deserved that cut from her.

"Are you still leaving?" he asked.

Her gaze softened. "Not for a while, I guess."

That was good enough for him.

But he kept thinking about Marvin. They had searched every room and closet and found no sign of him. But why did he feel that he might still be around?

60

Speaking to the police officer who showed up almost an hour later that night was the perfunctory, time-wasting exercise Nate had known it would be, but he and Leslie filed the report anyway. The officer gave no assurance that Danielle would be arrested, only that she would be questioned about the events of that night. The cop also seemed skeptical about Nate's claim of being drugged, brows furrowing as Nate related his story, but he dutifully noted the details in his report.

Nate didn't bother bringing up Marvin with the police. He had no evidence the guy had entered the house, and his personal, documented history with Marvin was spotty. Losing his cool the other day and getting arrested inadvertently created more complications when he wanted to engage the law on his behalf.

Besides, he was beginning to doubt Marvin had been there. As Leslie had insisted: it made no sense. Danielle had turned out to be as shady as her brother, but the siblings despised each other.

The only positive outcome to this long, nightmarish day was that Leslie had returned.

"Are you sure you don't want to go to the emergency room?" she asked. "I think you should."

They were in their master bedroom. Nate sat in an armchair in the sitting area while Leslie stood over him, scrutinizing the bump on his head.

"At this point, I've busted my nose and jacked up my hand, and now I've added a knot to my head. No, thanks, Les. I'll take two ibuprofen and call it a night."

"No, no." She clucked her tongue, in full mothering mode. "You should get it checked out. Hitting your head like you did could lead to serious complications later."

"Fine. I'll go to urgent care tomorrow and get some tests done."

"Hey." She gave him a direct look. "Don't say that only to shut me up. I'm serious."

Despite his discomfort, he laughed.

"What?" she asked.

"I'm really glad you're back home."

"Hmph. You should be."

"And I'm glad you believed me."

"Well, I wanted to strangle you at first."

"I'm glad you didn't act on that impulse, Les."

"I don't think I've ever been so pissed. Ever."

"I know it looked bad. I'm sorry. For everything. I hope you can forgive me."

He reached for her hand, which she allowed him to hold. He fitted the engagement ring back onto her finger.

Her eyes looked moist; his certainly were.

"I never lied to you," he said. "But I'm sorry for what I did."

"You're good at many things, but lying isn't one of them. That's one thing I know about you for sure. I had to get past my knee-jerk reaction and remember who you are."

"Thank you, Les. I love you to pieces, seriously."

"Love you too, babe." She touched his shoulder. "We should turn in. It's late, and it's been one heck of a day."

He turned toward the bed; the mattress looked inviting, and the sight of it triggered a yawn.

An unfamiliar, small, turquoise-colored item lay on Leslie's nightstand.

"What's that?" he asked.

"My pepper spray key chain. I'm keeping it close by until everything blows over. Call me paranoid if you want."

"Hmm. Not mad at you."

About an hour later, Nate still hadn't fallen asleep, though having Leslie beside him in bed helped him relax more than he had in days. The ibuprofen had taken the edge off his headache, leaving him with only a faint throbbing, but he was restless. The day's dramatic ups and downs had left him unable to switch off.

He did what he always did to unwind: headed to his office to do some work.

Downstairs, he found the door to the garage ajar a few inches, and he closed it as he shuffled past. He must've forgotten to shut it earlier when he'd retrieved something from his truck.

He switched on the lights in his office. Although Danielle hadn't stolen anything from the room, he felt violated knowing she had been there without his consent. What had she been looking for? A stash of cash lying around? A list of critical passwords? A key to their safe?

From the start, he had misread Danielle's intentions. Foolishly, he believed she was attracted to him and genuinely wanted to help, and receiving lavish attention from a beautiful woman had flattered his ego. She'd pulled the oldest trick in the book on him, and he'd fallen for it. In that respect, she and her con-man brother were more alike than he had realized.

Never again, he thought as he booted up his laptop.

Nevertheless, he would need to learn more about Danielle's family court remark. If she had somehow taken something precious from him while he was unconscious (the very idea turned his stomach), he would need to share that with Leslie, and they would need to figure out how to protect themselves.

But that was a problem for tomorrow.

He accessed the email account he used for business. Since he'd last checked earlier that afternoon, he had received a notification from the background screening company on the inquiry he had opened for Marvin a few days ago. The results had finally arrived.

Based on his prior discussions with Danielle about her brother, the report probably contained nothing noteworthy. By then, Nate understood that Marvin was a grifter with a lengthy arrest record and a score of unreported crimes.

Regardless, the screening firm would bill Nate for the investigation. Nate clicked on the link to access the case report. Sipping cold water from an insulated bottle, he leaned forward in his desk chair and studied the screen.

"Oh shit," he whispered and spat water on his lap.

Upstairs, Leslie screamed.

61

———

When Nate climbed out of bed, he unknowingly awoke Leslie, too.

Lying in the warm darkness, Leslie watched Nate shuffle out of the room and gently shut the door behind him. Knowing him as well as she did, Nate was restless and would go downstairs into his office to work for a while, to soothe his nerves.

She burrowed underneath the soft sheets, sighing with deep contentment despite experiencing one of the wildest days in recent memory.

She was glad she had come home. It was where she ought to be. Nate needed her, and in her way, she needed him, too. Although they could be strong as individuals, working together as a team allowed them to function at their best, and no challenge was too great for them to overcome.

There was still much for them to sort out with this Danielle situation. It would require patience, especially for her, because her first impulse was to let jealousy consume her, but in her soul, she knew Nate's heart—that was the important thing.

Of course, there was the Marvin problem, too. It bugged her how

Nate had been convinced earlier that the psycho was hiding in the house. He kept saying it, and it made her want to scream, and she was thankful when Nate finally dropped it.

But there was something she remembered from earlier. Something she needed to confirm.

She reached for her phone, which lay on the nightstand next to her miniature pepper spray key chain. The screen brightened.

She opened the Ring app. When she had looked earlier, the system was unavailable due to an internet outage.

The internet service had been restored. The camera app had stored history until the outage, which occurred around eight.

Leslie scrolled through the system notifications.

She was rewarded with doorbell cam footage of Danielle (*damn her, she's so pretty*) showing up at the front door, dressed to seduce. Nate told her to go away despite her pleadings, and something happened out of view, but the woman entered the house in the end.

The camera continued to record. A few seconds later, someone else followed Danielle inside.

Leslie gasped, her heart clutching.

Nate was right.

Across the room, the bedroom door whispered open. A shadowy figure invaded the room.

She bolted upright in bed and reached for the nightstand, her hand closing over the pepper spray.

The lights flared on, the sudden brightness disorienting her. The intruder closed the distance between them and pointed a gun at her head.

"Miss Lady," Marvin said.

Leslie screamed.

62

Upstairs, Leslie had screamed—a single shriek of pure terror. Nate erupted to his feet, the desk chair careening away behind him.

Dread wrapped around him in an icy sleeve.

I knew it. He's here.

The guy had waited hours. Where had he hidden? Where had they failed to look?

Doesn't matter now. Leslie's in danger.

Nate had left his phone upstairs in the bedroom, recharging on the nightstand for the night. Like many people these days who'd gone completely mobile for communications, he didn't keep a landline in the house.

His gun was upstairs, too, locked in the safe in the master bedroom closet. *Dammit.*

The only helpful weapon in the room was a piece of sports memorabilia: a baseball bat autographed by Hank Aaron hanging in a glass-fronted display case on the wall behind the printer.

Hands quivering, Nate unlatched the case lid and slid out the gleaming bat. The handle felt like ice in his clammy palms, but the hardwood possessed a satisfying weight.

He hurried out of the office and into the hallway.

The garage, he thought, with sudden certainty. Hadn't he discovered the connecting door ajar a few minutes ago? It was the one place they hadn't searched for him—they were so focused on rooms, closets, and other interior areas.

Too late for that now.

Nate crept to the base of the staircase and looked upward.

He didn't see anyone in the dimly lit hallway. Silence had taken over the house. Leslie hadn't screamed again, and he'd heard no other voices.

Maybe Les had a bad dream and popped out of it screaming.

But in his gut, he knew that wasn't true.

"Les?" he said. "Babe, are you okay?"

Only the house's ordinary groans and creaks answered.

Clutching the bat, the barrel balanced near his shoulder, he climbed the steps.

His heartbeat thundered. Adrenaline chimed through his blood: all his senses felt hyper-vivid, as keen as a hunter's on the prowl.

When he reached the top of the staircase, he turned the corner. At the end of the hallway, the master bedroom's double doors hung half-open. Pale yellow light spilled from within.

Breathing low and slow, Nate shouldered through the doors.

Leslie turned at his entrance. She sat upright on the bed, eyes wide and tears sliding down her cheeks, her hands gathered beneath the rumpled bedsheets.

A man sat on the mattress, positioned behind her. He held a handgun to Leslie's head; it looked like a Glock, the deadly black metal glinting in the light.

He grinned at Nate's arrival.

"Welcome to the party, Nathan," he said.

Nate squeezed the bat's handle.

"You're not Marvin," Nate said.

"Aww, shucks, brother." The intruder chuckled. "You finally ran that background check, did you? Marv and I always looked alike, but thirty years later, how would you know?"

63

Nate blinked cold sweat out of his eyes and glowered at the man holding Leslie at gunpoint. Nate started talking, struggling to make sense of this newest turn, desperate to delay violence until he could come up with a plan to save her life.

"The background check got a hit on your Social Security Number," Nate said. "You used your legit SSN even though you put 'Marvin Waters' on your job application. Your real birth name is Ian Hall. You changed it legally to Bediako Seidu eight years ago. That's the name you were under when I bailed you out of jail. Danielle told me to use it 'cause she said Marvin had changed his name to an African one. I never questioned it."

"You're a good brother, you know that?" Ian said. "Straight up, I respect that about you. You were willing to give a felon a legit shot, no tough questions asked, no background check off the jump."

"Put the gun down, please," Nate said. "No one needs to get hurt here. We can talk like reasonable people."

Ian rose from the bed, but he kept the pistol levered against Leslie's head. Her jaws clenched, Leslie squeezed her eyes shut, as if trying to wish away this nightmare.

"Got your phones, bro." Ian patted his jacket pocket. "We're gonna finish our business tonight, with no more interruptions from anyone."

Nate glanced at the nightstand and confirmed the man was telling the truth. His iPhone was gone, and he must have taken Leslie's, too.

"Now, look, I *knew* Marv," Ian said. "We got tight in juvie. He told me all about you, Nathan. Bike rides and video games." Ian snickered. "And yeah, he told me about that fucked-up letter you wrote that his psycho stepdaddy blamed on him. He never forgave you for that shit. Good job, kid."

"Where is Marvin?" Nate asked. "The real Marvin?"

Ian's eyes glinted, but he shrugged. "Dead."

The answer hit Nate like a dull blow to the chest. Marvin, dead? All this time?

"But Danielle—" Nate started.

"She's my lady, dude, on and off—mostly off, now. Marv hooked us up years ago. She's fine as wine, but the girl's got issues. Did she ever tell you what she did to her mama?"

Nate edged closer to the bed, still holding the bat. Closing the gap and keeping this psychopath babbling might get him within striking distance.

He shifted his gaze from the man to Leslie. Leslie kept her tearful gaze fastened on Nate, and he could sense, perhaps through a telepathic bond, that she understood his intent. He saw her hands burrowed under the bed covers fidget.

"Danielle told me she didn't get along with her mother," Nate said.

"Didn't get along?" Ian snorted. "Shit, Danny pushed the bitch down the stairs. Everyone thought it was an accident. Danny got the insurance money."

"She killed her mother?" Leslie whispered. "Lord have mercy."

"But I'm here to get paid," Ian said. "That's been the deal all along. We've taken the scenic route to get here, but that's where we've landed, fam. Marvin Waters wants what you owe him for fucking up his life." He laughed.

"It was always a con?" Nate asked. "This whole guilt trip you laid on me?"

As he spoke to Ian, he inched closer. Less than ten feet separated them.

"Pause right there." Ian switched the pistol's aim from Leslie to Nate and stepped away from the bed. "I don't want to shoot anybody, fam, but my Glock is locked and loaded, and I'll put your ass down like a dog in the street. Don't try me." He cut his gaze at Leslie. "That means you, too, Miss Lady. Don't move."

Nate halted in mid-step. Leslie watched them, frozen in place, shuddering.

"Chill, okay?" Nate said. "You said you want money, right? Let's talk then."

Keeping the gun aimed at Nate, Ian slid something out of his pocket: a pair of steel-plated handcuffs.

"I want three things." Ian wiggled the cuffs. "Number one: you're going to put down the bat and cuff your lady to the bedpost here so we can get her out of the way, and you're taking me to the safe in your closet and cracking it open."

"There's nothing in there," Nate said.

"You're no good at lying. You're too honest of a dude to sell it. Don't bother."

Nate's heart slammed. "You asked me to give you a car."

"Fuck the car," Ian said: "'Cause, look, here's step number two: you're going to transfer funds to my Bitcoin wallet. Everything you got."

"Bitcoin? I don't have any Bitcoin, man."

"Didn't I already tell you that you suck at lying? You *told* me you dabbled in it, and I saw the file in your office. You got a sweet slice of them coins and you're giving it all up."

Nate had purchased Bitcoin several years ago, buying a small share of the cryptocurrency more as a lark than a serious money-making venture, but the value of his stake had climbed over the years to a high, five-figure sum. He'd never sold any of it. On some level, the crypto craze didn't seem real; it felt more like a game than legitimate investing, and he wanted to see where it would all wind up in the end.

Bitcoin was infamously difficult to trace if stolen, and letting his holdings wind up in this grifter's pocket meant that money would be gone for good. But he'd give it all up if it meant saving Leslie.

"Number three," Ian said. "You're going to write a letter for *me*."

"A . . . a letter?"

"You'll write me a letter of recommendation. I may want to apply for a new job somewhere someday. Having a steady gig is always a nice cover story, and who better to pen me a letter than my highly respected business owner pal?"

"You're out of your mind," Nate said. "If I do everything you're telling me to do, the cops will be all over your ass as soon as you walk out of the house. You won't get to spend a penny of those bitcoins."

"I know how to dip out of sight till the heat cools off, man, and Danny isn't a snitch, though we've been butting heads the whole time on this damn job. The typical woman always wanting to get her way." Ian glanced at Leslie and sneered. "You're like that, too, Miss Lady. Bossy ass bitch."

Leslie trembled but said nothing.

"You won't get away with this," Nate said.

"Drop the bat right there on the floor." Ian pointed with the pistol. "Then get over here and cuff your lady to the bedpost. Move it, Nathan." He made a hurry-up gesture with the handgun.

Nate stared at Ian, but in the corner of his eye, he noticed Leslie grasping something underneath the bedsheets.

And he thought he knew what it might be.

All he needed to do was provide a distraction. Something Ian wouldn't expect. Something surprising.

You're a good brother, you know that?

All his life, people assumed Nate would behave as the good guy.

The reliable fellow who always did the reasonable things, followed all the rules, checked all the boxes, saw the best in everyone, and avoided risks; his trustworthy nature might have been his greatest strength, but it was his Achilles' heel, too. Because of it, Ian had exploited him from the start; so had Danielle.

It had all led Nate to this moment, a point in time that could define the rest of his life. He saw that now.

He clutched the bat handle.

"No," Nate said. "I'm not doing anything for you. I've had enough. Go ahead and kill me."

Ian had been watching Nate with a twisted, cocky grin. But his smile faltered, and in his apparent bewilderment, he lowered the gun a few inches.

It was the opportunity Leslie needed.

64

————

The past several minutes had been the wildest of Leslie's life, a fitting finale for a crazy day.

All along, she and Nate believed they had been dealing with Nate's childhood best friend, Marvin. But the old friend was dead, and this man in their room was a stranger. It was enough to make her question everything else she thought she knew.

But one thing was clear: she would get only one shot to take advantage of a slipup.

While Nate talked to this stranger, Leslie tightened her hold on her pepper spray, which she managed to hide underneath the bedsheets when Ian first invaded the room, though he had taken her phone. She and Nate exchanged glances, and she read his thoughts: *When I give you an opening, Les, you know what to do.*

"No," Nate said to Ian. "I'm not doing anything for you. I've had enough. Go ahead and kill me."

Nate's stunning answer to Ian's demands hit the guy like cold water in his smug face, and he allowed his gun to dip—and he was ignoring Leslie, too, like she didn't matter.

She snatched the pepper spray from underneath the covers and sprayed Ian's eyes. A stream of orangish fluid spattered him.

Ian let out a garbled scream and clapped his hand to his face. "Fuck!"

Things happened quickly then.

Nate rushed across the room with the baseball bat, unleashing a battle cry. He swung the bat at Ian like a slugger going for the fences.

Although blinded, Ian was already spinning away. The bat smacked into his shoulder. He yelped in pain, and the impact knocked him off balance.

But he didn't fall.

And he didn't drop the gun.

Still whirling like a top, deprived of clear sight, Ian squeezed the trigger. The sound of gunfire in the bedroom was like a detonating bomb, shredding Leslie's eardrums.

The round punched through the bedframe, only inches away from her, splinters flying and peppering her face.

But he kept shooting. Wildly.

Leslie dove off the bed and toward the floor like a woman hurling herself into a pool, instinctively trying to put herself out of range.

As she leaped, a sharp pressure twanged through her left shoulder. She'd never felt anything like it in her life, but a terrible realization passed through her.

Oh, Jesus, I've been shot.

65

Despite the pepper spray Leslie had used on Ian's eyes, the blinded madman fired the Glock multiple times. Nate's ears rang from the close-quarters gunfire, and he might have been shot—he was so high on adrenaline, he didn't know. But he swung the bat again with all the strength left in him, intent on caving in Ian's skull like a watermelon.

The bat smashed into Ian's head with a sickening crack.

Ian collapsed to the floor as if a manhole had popped open beneath him. The pistol flipped out of his fingers.

Nate gulped in deep breaths. His lungs ached from panting, and the bat seemed to vibrate in his fingers from the aftereffects of the blow he had delivered. The acrid odor of gunpowder thickened the air.

Miraculously, Nate had avoided getting shot. But Leslie was sprawled on the carpet. Blood spread from her shoulder, blooming like a terrible rose on her nightgown.

No, no, no, no, no.

Nate grabbed the gun off the floor and scrambled toward her. He cradled her in his arms.

Her eyelids fluttered, and her gaze found his. Her lips quivered, but only wordless gasps of shock escaped her.

Frantic, Nate checked her pulse and found it beating rapid and strong, a good sign. But how long would it last?

After all they had been through, he couldn't lose her. Not like this. Life dealt a losing hand sometimes, but it couldn't be this cruel.

"Hang on, baby," Nate said. "Just hang on, please. I'm gonna get you help, baby."

Behind them, groaning, Ian clambered to his feet. Like a man wobbling home after a long night of heavy drinking, he seesawed across the bedroom, colliding against furniture. He stumbled through the doorway.

Nate searched the nightstand for Leslie's phone and remembered: the asshole Ian had both their cells. Shit.

He snatched a pillow off the bed and gently pressed it against Leslie's shoulder, where she appeared to have been wounded based on the amount of blood seeping out of her. She uttered a thin cry and gritted her teeth, determination flashing in her eyes.

"Keep this here," Nate whispered. He positioned her slack fingers around the pillow. His chest was tight, and he realized he was sobbing. "I'll be right back."

"You . . . better . . ." she said through her tears.

Nate got to his feet. He clasped the Glock in both hands. His palms were sticky with sweat.

He was a business owner, not a trained soldier, cop, or gun enthusiast. The extent of his firearms experience was a long-ago weekend class at a self-defense retreat and the occasional, rare visit to the local firing range.

But Leslie depended on him.

He advanced across the bedroom to the wide doorway.

The hallway ahead was empty. A glance downstairs confirmed the front door was closed; Nate had engaged the security system before heading to bed. An alarm would have been triggered if the front or rear exterior doors were opened.

Unless Ian had shattered a window and crawled outside, he was in the house. But where?

Every passing second was precious.

"Ian!" Nate shouted in a raspy voice. "Get out here and face me like a man!"

No response.

Nate heard clattering on the roof. A steady rainfall had begun. Thunder rumbled in the distance.

Nate noticed faint, orangish-red droplets trailing across the hallway carpet. They were remnants of the pepper spray Leslie had used on Ian. But the liquid trail led to several closed doors off the corridor. Ian could have taken cover in any of them.

Nate would have to check each one.

The nearest room, on the left, was a bathroom. Clasping the pistol in his right hand, Nate used his left to twist the doorknob. Then he kicked the door open. It banged against the adjacent wall.

Darkness greeted him, broken only by the outline of the vanity and the bathtub, which had its curtain drawn.

Nate stepped inside and raked his hand over the light switch, flooding the room with brightness. He ripped aside the curtain.

No one was in there.

This is crazy. Go faster. Leslie needs you.

He steadied his grip on the Glock, swung back to the doorway, and stepped toward it.

Yelling, Ian charged him.

He flung something at Nate's face, a big white fluttery thing that Nate crazily thought at first was a massive bird, but it was only a bath towel.

It landed on Nate's face, cloaking him in sudden darkness.

Desperate and blind, Nate squeezed the Glock's trigger.

Ian snarled with agony. "Motherfucker, you shot me!"

Nate yanked the towel off his head. Ian was up close, only inches away, rage burning in his reddened, swollen eyes. He gripped something that flashed silver in the hallway light. He swiped it at Nate.

The switchblade slashed across Nate's breastbone, leaving a trail of fire.

Gasping, weakened, Nate tried to maneuver the pistol for another shot. Ian seized his arm and attempted to wrestle away the gun.

Grappling with each other, they grunted and cursed. Ian got the upper hand and slammed Nate against the hallway wall. The collision knocked the breath out of Nate's lungs. Nearby, a framed photo rattled and dropped to the floor.

The gun slipped out of Nate's fingers and thudded to the carpet, too.

"Soft as cotton," Ian muttered.

He hammered his fist into Nate's face, pounding Nate's already fractured nose. Nate felt bones pop, a sensation like glass shards exploding in his nostrils. White stars wheeled in his vision.

Ian kicked away the gun.

"Gonna pay me, motherfucker." Ian punched him deep in the stomach. "Gonna give me everything you got."

Choking on blood and pain, Nate doubled over. As he reeled against the wall, Ian pressed his knife against Nate's throat.

"Making this so goddamn hard, and it's all so simple," Ian said. "Now we're gonna go back in there and open the fuckin' safe, all right? Getting back to step motherfuckin' one."

Leslie, Nate thought. *No, no, no.*

"I want you to crawl in there like a dog." Ian tapped the blade against Nate's cheek. "Go on, man. Get to crawling."

Nate felt warm blood seeping from the knife wound opened in his chest. How bad was it? It couldn't be worse than what Leslie had suffered . . . his fiancée, bleeding out in the bedroom, relying on him to get help.

Nate gritted his teeth and lunged. He swung his elbow against Ian's knee—the injured one.

Ian's knee cracked and buckled. He let out a ragged howl of agony.

Nate surged to his feet and shoved Ian toward the staircase. Ian plummeted backward, his mouth gaping wide in an "O" of shock.

The sound of him crashing down the steps echoed like thunder through the house.

Shaking and bleeding, Nate stumbled to the head of the stairs. Ian lay at the bottom, neck contorted, his twitching limbs bent at unnatural angles. Blood stained his pants leg, perhaps from when Nate had squeezed off a blind shot.

Was he dead?

Nate realized he didn't care.

Nate clutched the railing for support and plodded down the steps. As he closed in on Ian, he saw the man's chest rising and falling—he was alive, only knocked out from the fall down the stairs.

Nate fished the mobile phones from Ian's jacket pocket and called 911.

AFTER

Eight weeks later, Nate and Leslie wed in a church ceremony officiated by her longtime pastor and attended by a select circle of close friends and family. Afterward, they held a dinner reception at their favorite Italian restaurant.

"I know this isn't the Big Day you had in mind," Nate told Leslie. He sat beside her at the long banquet table heaped with delicious food. He kissed her cheek; since her recovery from the gunshot wound to her shoulder, he could hardly keep his hands off her. "I hope you're not disappointed."

In fact, the pared-down wedding had been Leslie's idea. After surviving that fateful night when they'd skated along the edge of death, she confessed she already had been thinking about priorities; in the larger scheme of things, an opulent wedding, though a childhood dream, wasn't as meaningful to her as she had once believed.

Nevertheless, Nate felt a twinge of guilt. This was the small, intimate affair he'd wanted all along.

"Don't forget—there's always the vow renewal." Smiling, Leslie patted his hand. "We'll do it big then. I'm not letting you totally off the hook, buddy. You better be here in ten years."

"I'm not going anywhere, babe." He kissed her again.

They honeymooned in Grand Cayman for seven nights. Nate had promised to avoid checking work email and to let all business calls route to voicemail, and even he was surprised that he managed to keep his word.

Perhaps seeing that scar across his chest from Ian's knife was a valuable reminder of what mattered most in life.

When they returned home, he needed to conclude one final piece of business.

On a clear Saturday morning in late April, he drove alone to Macon, Georgia. There, he found his destination in the city: a rambling, wooded park with a paved bicycle trail.

He had brought his road bike. He hadn't used the thing in years and wiped a layer of dust off the frame before he loaded it in the truck's flatbed.

He hauled the bicycle out of the vehicle and pushed it across the parking lot toward a small pavilion with benches and tables clustered in shadows beneath a steel canopy.

The man he planned to meet had already arrived. He sat at a table, his bike leaning on its kickstand.

As Nate neared, Marvin Waters rose to meet him.

Ian Hall, being the pathological liar he was, had lied about his old friend. Marvin wasn't dead, but he had chosen a new path after his mother's death.

Illness had kept Marvin from attending his mom's funeral—one of the few things Ian had said that was true. Her passing hit him so hard that he resolved to clean up his life.

Nate was grateful to Charlene Livingston, Marvin's aunt, for reconnecting him with his childhood friend.

Face-to-face after thirty years, the two men studied each other.

"You know what?" Nate said. "There's a resemblance, but you don't look *that* much like him. He was stretching the truth about that, too."

Marvin laughed. "It's good to see you, Nathan."

The men embraced.

They had spoken twice on the phone before their planned meeting. Nate had filled him in on everything that had happened; Marvin was in the dark, having severed the toxic connections from his past, including his old partner in crime, Ian, and his sister, Danielle. He enjoyed a quiet, fulfilling life as an HVAC technician and youth mentor at his church, and he didn't maintain a social media account because he feared someone from his troubled younger days would contact him.

Nate relayed to him that both his sister and her sometime lover were in jail, facing a long series of charges. As often occurred, the grifters had turned against each other in attempts to negotiate lesser sentences. Still, both faced significant prison time for major felonies: Danielle for her mother's decade-ago homicide and Ian for his attempted murder of Nate and Leslie.

Danielle's unseemly plan to get pregnant using sperm she'd stolen from Nate had failed, too, which Nate counted as a blessing.

Most importantly, Marvin shared with Nate that he had long ago forgiven him for his well-meaning intervention in his family's life when they were kids. *You had good intentions, Nathan, but you can't save everyone. Let it go. I already did.*

"I see you brought your bike, Nathan," Marvin said. "It looks dusty."

"I can still smoke you, man." Nate smiled.

Marvin's eyes gleamed. "Is that a bet?"

"Yup."

Marvin climbed on his bike. Nate hopped on his, too.

"The trail starts over there." Marvin pointed to a sign in the distance. He winked. "Try to keep up."

"Let's ride."

Laughing, the two friends raced each other through the park.

HEAR MORE FROM BRANDON

Did you enjoy this novel? Visit www.brandonmassey.com now to sign up for Brandon Massey's free mailing list. Mailing list members get advance news on the latest releases, the chance to win autographed copies in exclusive contests, and much more. Your email address will never be shared and you can unsubscribe at any time.

ABOUT BRANDON MASSEY

Brandon Massey was born June 9, 1973, and grew up in Zion, Illinois. He lives with his family near Atlanta, Georgia, where he is at work on his next novel. Visit his web site at www.brandon-massey.com for the latest news on his upcoming books.